Time and Place

stories and parables

DAVID ROWE

Gweithdy'r Gair
gweithdy@yahoo.com

Copyright © 2023 David Rowe

All rights reserved.

ISBN: *9 798395 672476*

for Ann

*and with sincere thanks
for their friendly criticism to*

*Ann Morgan
&
Paul Wright*

*and with special thanks to Paul,
an expert and very patient editor*

CONTENTS

The Happiest Man Ever Hanged	1
Lust and the Megalith	26
A Very Boring Day	45
Amputation	73
Game Over	88
Person or Persons Unknown	99
The Tussie-Mussie	115
Travellers	136
The House	192

The Happiest Man Ever Hanged

A fanciful parable

In the thick mud under the water, eggs lay, biding their time. Ugly grey nymphs skulked and hunted in this seething sludge. It seemed impossible that in a few short weeks they would climb up the stem of a weed, shed their shells, and dart away over the glistening water on flashing wings of gossamer.

The stream, which had raced down from the hills, meandered through the flat grassy meadows, bubbled over the stepping-stones and swirled around rocks. When the tide was out, the stream was narrow and the mud exposed, but when the tide crept in, the valley bottom was covered with brackish water.

On the left bank, a few huts were clustered around a spring. A hundred yards further on, a large house perched on the hill that dominated the valley.

On the far side of the river, a curlew picked its way along, poking under stones, sorting through silt. A heron glided onto the bank and stood on the edge of the faster-running currents. With a yellow flash, a wagtail danced, curtseying gaily to the glistening stream.

Gwilym ducked and bobbed like the wagtail, stalked like the heron. He did not notice that his shoes, his trousers, everything was wet and covered in mud. It was not certain that he recognised a difference between earth and water, that he knew he could not just walk out into the river.

"Gwilym, where are you?"

Spring

It was not possible to watch him all the time.

Although he was fully grown, his body was curiously smooth and rounded, with plump, unshaped limbs like those of a baby. He was strong, too strong for his own good. He could get into situations that he could not get out of. He could not reason any more than he could speak.

He grunted a lot, and some people maintained that he was trying to speak. Others argued that not only could he not speak, but also that he couldn't understand what was said to him any more than a dog could. Many, especially those who had dogs, found this comparison inappropriate.

He did not think about the future or remember the past. He was an innocent whose ability to enjoy life made him sadly unfitted for life.

It needed only a moment's inattention. He would follow anything: a child, a bird, a sigh, a flash of light, a smell, a fairy seed dancing on the breeze. And in an instant, he would be out of sight.

At this time of year there was too much work to do, and his mother could not afford to lose so much time. The earth had to be scratched, the seeds to be planted, to be watered. The water had to be fetched from the spring, bucket by back-breaking bucket.

And every day, before going to her work, she had to pull out the weeds, so that the sun would scorch their roots: endless, inevitable weeds that pushed their sinister white tentacles deep down into her life.

And Gwilym had to be washed, dressed, fed and let out for a while.

"Gwilym!" she called.

It would have been easier to tie him up, but she would not do it. She would have been aware of the indignity, even if his simplicity protected him from such abstract suffering.

And she always hoped that she would not lose him, would not have to hurry wearily down to the river.

For that was where he would be. That was where he always was: sitting, waiting, watching, making low, gurgling noises almost like those of a purring cat.

She picked her way among the reeds, fighting back tears when her feet slipped into the water or were sucked in by the mud.

"Gwilym!"

He stood up, waving happily.

"Didn't I tell you not to ...?" she shouted with relief. Tears of pain shone in her eyes as the weight bore down on her. She brushed them away with the back of her dry, dusty, withered hand.

She was too old. She was worn out by childbearing and work and sickness and hunger. Worn out by life! Too old, too weak, too tired, too alone. Her man had died, her other children had left: some were dead, some were crushed by their own life.

If only Gwilym would leave, she thought, she also could die. She chased away this crippling self-pity. If only he could leave!

"Come on," she said quietly, and took him by the hand.

The House

A vast fireplace took up the whole wall at the far end of the kitchen. Pots of different sizes hung from hooks over a log fire, and spits with birds and small game on them were turned in the scorching heat. Steam from the cauldrons rose in swirls inside the chimney, and the bubbling of the contents of the pots could be heard over the crackle of the fire itself. Now and again, flames shot up as fat from the roasting meat fell on the fire.

On racks in front of the fire, sauces and broths were being kept hot until the time to use them came. On shelves around the walls and hanging from hooks in the ceiling beams, a vast array of utensils gleamed.

Meats were being cut up; vegetables and fruits were being cleaned; fowl were being gutted, the innards being passed to others who prepared them in a dozen different ways. There was the noise of the fire, of spitting fat, of small animals waiting to be slaughtered, and of children playing, fighting, crying.

It was like a gruesome festival where the edible dead were celebrated. Nothing was too big or too small to escape the appetites of the House. Everything waited to be prepared and devoured.

The cook patrolled, inspecting each task, shouting instructions. He inspired fear in all around him, for an unfavourable judgement on the cleanliness of an intestine, or the adequacy with which a liver had been chopped, meant instant dismissal. If not worse!

Not that they were well rewarded for their labour. But they were fed. Or rather they were allowed what was left on the platters when they came back from the dining room. And they were allowed to live in huts in the village and to cultivate a patch of land. Of course, much of the produce from that patch would go to the House as tribute, but there would be something left for them. Usually.

She was working, along with half a dozen other women, at a table that ran for much of the length of the room. She was making the sauce for the roast swan. She scooped entrails and blood from a pail, and poured them carefully over a lump of stale bread in the bottom of a pan. She took the liver and chopped it up finely. She put the pot over the fire, and waited for the cook, as only he was allowed to add cinnamon or sugar until it was to his satisfaction.

All around her, people were busy. There was the wine to be watered; the pastry to be made; bread to be baked. Peacocks, hares, pigeons, rabbits, bitterns, quince, apples, eagles, medlars, snipe, carp, beans, cabbage, gooseberries, plums, cowslips, marigolds, lamprey: it seemed that the whole of creation was to be devoured.

Sometimes the Master, who thought of himself as being close to his people, indeed as one of the people, might wander through, dipping a finger in this sauce, pulling a piece of meat from that joint, nodding at one woman, smiling at another, encouraging them all, for, as he tried to make these lumpen creatures understand, the good of the House meant the good of the people.

With greasy fingers they would tug their forelocks, curtsey, mumble, and continue the never-ending task of feeding him, as the meek dunnock is compelled to feed the cuckoo.

Damselflies

Gwilym crouched motionless, one arm outstretched. He had seen the brilliant streaks of colour, the cobweb wings, the huge iridescent eyes of a dragonfly: those brief witnesses of the summer's heat.

He would wait. Perhaps for a minute, perhaps for an hour. He could not tell.

But perhaps a sparkling streak of viridian would settle on his hand, and gossamer wings with glossy cobalt patches would flick open and closed, as if panting in the heat, wings like those of angels, shimmering in the breeze.

He whispered to the flitting streaks of colour, to the sighing grasses, to the glistening water, to the hum and drone of a million forms of life and death.

Another damselfly would dart by, and the first would

follow, dipping and diving among the waving grass. Sometimes a male would seize a female, bend her to their elemental wills, and, locked in a primeval embrace, like some ancient cabalistic symbol, they would move across the water, eggs and sperm sinking into the slime.

"Gwilym," she called.

And it would all start over.

"Gwilym," she cried. And she took his hand to lead him back.

The sun was well clear of the horizon, and the dew had been burned off. The plot would not be weeded that morning. As she worked at the House, the weeds would grow, their strangely pale roots sucking from the earth the water that she had struggled to carry. Second by second, minute by minute, hour by hour, they would grow, and each leaf, each shoot, each parasitic cell diminished her. For a moment she stood still, her eyes screwed up tight with pain and despair. Why could he not ...?

She stopped, suddenly panic-stricken. She looked around, spinning on the spot, taking one step in one direction, and then taking two steps back. She did not have the hoe.

"Stay there", she shouted.

He smiled gently, lifted his arms, waved them up and down slowly, rhythmically, in time with the damselfly that he could still see in his head.

It was no use. By the time she had turned her back he would have disappeared again. She grabbed his hand, and pulled him after her as she hurried back.

She retraced in her mind every step, every time she had called out, every single moment, -except the one when the hoe had dropped from her hand.

She despatched some children who were playing by the stream along the path or down into the water, while she scurried backwards and forwards as quickly as her age would permit.

She pulled him along the path behind her, the tears streaming down her face.

It was no use. She could not survive without the hoe, but she had to go to the House.

She could not afford the luxury of staring at her own misery. When she had done her work and returned from the House, when she had taken Gwilym out, when she had worked on the plot as best she could, when she had made their food, when she had finally got her child to bed, then, in the brief darkness before the dawn, when she should have been sleeping, then she would be able to worry about how she would manage to pay her tribute and to feed them both. In her fitful sleep, her dreams would conjure up a future even worse than the present.

The First Time

The first time it happened nobody paid that much attention. Most maintained that it was no more than fortuitous coincidence. Some wondered if it was an unwonted and benign intervention by the gods.

Perhaps it was just that damselflies really did bring good luck, as some believed.

She had been everywhere, searched among the reeds

and the rocks, between the roots of trees and bushes.

If he was a judgement on her, then she must have been very evil. He was a sentence, not of death, but of life, of life beyond its due time.

When a mayfly dies on its first summer evening, it does not berate some divinity because of its modest portion of life. Why would it want another day? It had done what it had to do.

So had she. She had been born, reproduced, fed and fought for her children, and now she should have been able to die. Yet when she had already run her course, when he should have been a man with his own children to look after, she had to struggle to look after him.

"Gwilym!" she called out.

He was crouching among the sighing grasses, silent, with the waving webs of light of a damselfly perched on his outstretched hand.

"The hoe, Gwilym," she whispered.

He blew softly on his hand and the damselfly flew away. Before she could stop him, he ran after it, chasing along the river, splashing in and out of the water, causing a cloud of insects to rise into the evening air.

"Gwilym," she called.

"Gwilym," she wept.

The damselfly dropped to the water where, for a few seconds, its body glistened like a jewel, before the current swept it away.

Gwilym stared uncomprehendingly. Then he stooped

and picked up the hoe which lay at his feet.

The story was told and retold. For a few days. the villagers spoke of little else. When Gwilym was taken down to the plot in the mornings and in the evenings, neighbours would stare narrowly as he went by. They even knew about it at the House. The Master had commented on her good fortune. It was not easy for her, he had said, but we cannot presume to understand the blessings of the gods.

And he went on his way, smiling and greeting, noting in his mind the best cabbages, the ripest fruits, the plumpest animals that he would claim as his tribute.

The women were less inclined to believe in the gods, certainly less inclined to think that the gods, assuming for the moment that there were any, ever bothered themselves with human affairs. And certainly not to give a helping hand. It was a mere fluke.

Of course, they were all pleased that it had happened. There was no question about that. But it would be a mistake to read anything into it. It was a fluke. Pure coincidence. Luck. Good fortune.

Responsibility

It was not easy to be in charge. When the ordinary people finished work, they could relax and enjoy themselves. They could go to a feast, get drunk, dance, mate and sleep the sleep of the simple. He would have to plan. Who else would organise the ordinary people, make them productive, protect them from those who would use them, abuse them? Who else would decide who was a friend, who a foe? Who would arrange the hunting and the fishing and the harvests? Who would find the right wife for his eldest son, a wife who would breed, be faithful and bring a dowry?

He was negotiating with a neighbour, but the deal was not made as yet. Careful thought was required. There were principles, strategies, tactics to take into consideration.

No, they were like a large family, and he was the head. What would happen to the bees if they did not feed the queen? He was responsible. It was his right and his duty.

Lightning strikes twice

Life went back to normal: the plots, the river, the Master. They did not question their life, for they knew of no other life, and could not imagine any other. They all performed a function, and occasionally they courted, reproduced and, of course, died.

The event was classified, but not forgotten, for nothing is forgotten there. "Gwilym and the hoe" took its place along with the deaths of children, an eclipse of the moon, a good harvest, a flood, a hot summer, snowfall, the meaning of lightning, the uses of herbs and the lists of fifth cousins.

Despite the saying, people are well aware that lightning does strike twice, although such an occurrence does not necessarily mean that the gods wish to communicate any message in such a repetition. Of course, the odds against such a coincidence are pretty long, but while it may be improbable, the very act of calculating its improbability proves its possibility.

And although some of them had dismissed the suggestion as plain stupid, others pointed out that they had nothing to lose.

So the villagers went along to where Gwilym was sitting happily in the plot as his mother was collecting the last of the beans.

"A ewe has wandered off," they explained, "and we cannot find her. We wondered …."

Their voices tailed off, as if unable or unwilling to put such a foolish idea into words. But they turned to Gwilym who was hopping around most seriously in the company of a chaffinch.

"Perhaps if Gwilym could …. We will finish collecting the beans for you."

Gwilym seemed not to listen, certainly not to understand when they told him of the missing ewe. Yet as soon as he was free, he raced off, arms spread like wings, running through the fields with a tail of villagers hurrying behind.

The ewe had her head stuck in the branches of a thorn bush and could not free herself.

Gwilym's mother slept well that night, and, in the morning, she found a pan of broth and a bag of nuts at her door.

Probably it would have stopped there had chance not taken a hand again. People had come to accept that Gwilym could find things. Nobody could understand how he did it, but then, they didn't understand why the tide came in, or why the seasons changed, but that didn't stop anything.

But then the neighbour's sow was sick. Nothing seemed to work. Gwilym went out into the woods, picked leaves and berries, pulled up roots and brought them all back.

Again some said it was ridiculous. But the sow recovered.

Perhaps it was just a coincidence, but such a happy one, such an unexpected one! And much more important than a hoe. Some superstitious people even said it was a miracle.

The Death of a Dragonfly

As autumn approached, and the cold mists took hold of the land, animals and people, as always at that season, sickened. A cough, a strained muscle, a fever, the usual ailments saw more gifts being brought to Gwilym's mother, and more cures produced by Gwilym, cures that were no more understood than his ability to find things was. When he cured a child who was feverish and breathing with difficulty, who seemed beyond hope, many doubted no more, came to ask openly for Gwilym's help, brewed up his mixtures and celebrated the patient's recovery.

They just had to put the problem to Gwilym in such a way that he could reply, not with words, but with action.

Gwilym's reward was that when he was not needed, he was allowed to spend his days by the river. His mother would sit at the foot of a tree, watching him. At times she dozed off in the pale sun and had to go along the banks until she found him again.

He watched everything: ducks, circling kites, a magpie chasing a weasel, a cormorant locked in a comical struggle with an eel, if the struggle for life can ever be comical, a buzzard that had fallen in the water and which floated with ludicrous dignity, sitting upright like some aged queen on a throne.

And above all, he watched the dragonflies. He waited, hand outstretched among the reeds, until that flash of colour might alight. Then it was as if he too could fly on impossibly fragile wings that looked less substantial than air itself.

One day, as she slumbered by the tree in the sun, she heard a splash. Gwilym was in the water, trying to reach out into the current. She urged him out of the river, grabbed his arms, pulled him back. The tears were rolling down his face.

In the circling current, amidst a swirling circle of leaves, twigs, seeds and feathers, a brown and yellow dragonfly lay on the water, unable to beat its wings. For a few seconds it would struggle, and then it would drift around with the other debris. The wings that should have carried it away now prevented its escape. Gwilym stared, distraught, as its agony circled before his eyes. Round and round, struggling, resting, the wings becoming wetter, weaker, heavier.

It could not fly, but it was so light that it could not drown. The agony would end only when the body gave in to exhaustion, when it gave in to what had to be.

The tragedy was not that death came, but that it came in such a way.

The Feast

The women were busy: some tearing the legs off crabs, emptying the shells, putting all the meat into a dish with butter, cinnamon, sugar and vinegar; others making broth, boiling rosemary and thyme in water and wine, adding chickens, raisins and prunes and boiling again until the meat was cooked. Minced beef, roast venison, eels in butter and vinegar, tripe in red wine, borage flowers mixed with egg yolks, apples and curds: dish after dish was carried in by servants in their best livery. Wine, beer, cider, everything was served liberally. The musicians played.

The sticking point was the corn mill. If he could get that, not only would he have the income from grinding all the corn of the land, but he would control the river from the House to the sea.

The deal would be clinched, so the Master had planned, by the triumphant arrival of the cook's speciality: woodcock. The birds had been carefully plucked, their feathers like autumn leaves on the kitchen floor. They were gutted, but the liver had to be left in place, stuffed with lard and juniper berries. The birds' long bills were put into the breast, and the legs and feet were drawn up the sides. Toasted bread was laid in pans, and the woodcocks were placed on the toast. A sauce of white wine, parsley, ginger, salt and vinegar and fat from the roasting meat was poured over the birds.

The servants were lined up, the musicians played a rousing fanfare, and the dish was carried in.

The deal was concluded: the mill would be his. The wedding date was set for the end of the year.

A Child

The children were down by the river, catching elvers or stalking easy prey.

One child was playing high up past the huts, sailing a fine ship made of twigs and leaves and cobwebs. The ship moved proudly, the breeze filling its sails of leaves. The child watched it sweep around shallows, ride rapids, catch for a moment on a rock and then, in a disdainful swirl, resume its majestic journey. Down the reed-covered banks, past the stepping-stones, under the bridge, past the leet, among the gravel beds where sea trout came to spawn. He gave a captain's salute to Gwilym who was sitting by the stream talking to the cygnets, braving the angry swans who did not like this interference with their young. The ship sailed down into the marshes where the tide swept in, down to the rushing water by the rocks, down towards the estuary and on out of sight, surviving every peril. The finest ship ever to sail the mighty seas.

When he had not returned by nightfall, the villagers went out to look for him. In the feeble glow of smoking lanterns, they searched, calling to him, their calls mingling with the sounds of night: fish jumping to escape fleas or otters; ducks squabbling; owls screeching; even the occasional howl of a wolf. Everything hunted, or was hunted.

They had to call off the search at dawn to go to their work. At another time they might have had permission to continue the search, but this was a busy day at the House: guests were expected, the neighbours whose daughter was to marry the Master's son.

No compromise could be made, the Master had said. He was no tyrant. He asked only for what was necessary to maintain the House, and, thus, to maintain the community. He was the hub. They were the spokes. If now and again the great wheel should seem to be jolted off course, then it could be righted if everybody pulled their weight. And if a spoke should fail, then it could be replaced. The loss of a child might be regrettable, but it was little compared to the well-being of the community.

Again that evening they organised themselves. Two tides had come in since the child had disappeared, so their hopes were tempered by growing fears. As they set out, it was still high tide, and many of the lower branches and roots were hidden under the water.

She had no choice. She took Gwilym to his favourite place on the bank, and, despite her principles, tied him to a tree.

They went beyond the marshes, around the bend, past the mill, right down to the sandy strip facing the sea. All without success. In the fading light, their calls were at times drowned by the wailing of the mother of the missing child.

When she got back, Gwilym was still tied up, as happy as ever. He was crouching among the waving grasses, his arms resting on his knees, hands upturned. The riverbank throbbed with the sounds of a myriad forms of life. A thrush sat in the top of a tree, blessing the evening with its song. Somewhere upstream, the piercing screech of a barn owl shattered the peace of the evening. Gwilym jumped to his feet excitedly when he heard it, tried to imitate its silent gliding flight.

She untied him. At least he was alive, not drowned somewhere along the river, or swept out to sea.

"Don't make me look for you like that one day. Do you understand, Gwilym?" and she wrapped him in her arms.

Gwilym saw the barn owl drifting silently along the stream. In a second he was off: down the slope to the stream, across the stepping stones, down the path among the hawthorn and alder, chasing the ghostly shape ahead of him.

"Gwilym," she called. Despite her tiredness she had to follow. She called to neighbours, who joined her in the chase.

Eventually they found him sitting on a low, overhanging branch, holding the child's arm to keep him clear of the water.

In their joy, the villagers paid no attention to Gwilym. The father raced forward, tried to pull the child from the water. He was alive! His feet were caught in roots. A neighbour took a deep breath, and again and again he went under until the child's feet were released, and he was carried away amid the shouting, cheering, laughing villagers.

A fire burned all night as they warmed the child, fed him, wrapped him in warm clothing. By morning the child was almost recovered.

Of course, each time the story was told it became ever more extraordinary. It seemed that the barn owl had circled over Gwilym, had screeched as it flew along, calling Gwilym on, had been sitting on the branch with Gwilym when the neighbours finally caught up.

"Maybe," one said.

"Perhaps," another said.

It even appeared that the boy had been underwater, quite dead, and had started breathing again only when Gwilym had lifted his head.

That, of course, was preposterous. Nevertheless, some listened carefully, wary, frightened, yet excited.

A lot of people scoffed. As if that simpleton was capable of anything! Just another fluke. The idiot was chasing the owl, and was called to by the child who heard him grunting as he ran past.

The kitchen buzzed with the story. The Master found one of the sauces over-salted, and was not at all pleased. Fortunately, the neighbours with the mill and the daughter did not notice, but when he summoned the cook after the meal, the threats in his polite words were clearly understood.

When she went down to her plot that evening, leading Gwilym by the hand, many neighbours greeted Gwilym with a smile. One child, who thought it funny to run around shouting and making owl noises, got a very smart clip on the ear from his mother and ran off howling.

Things slowly settled down, and life resumed its normal pace. In the evenings, everything was a little easier. The plants were now bigger and stronger than the weeds. Already fruit and vegetables had formed, berries were ripening. The year's chicks had fledged and were easy to catch, adding to the season's plenty, a plenty which the Master could not fully control.

Winter

Each morning, thick frosts covered the ground, and wood smoke hung sweetly in the air. Each morning, Gwilym would gurgle with pleasure at the brittle beauty of the sparkling, silver coated world and would rush out. Each morning, he was surprised and disappointed to find that this glistening beauty was cold and wet.

Winter is always the bad time. There were no more berries, no more fruit, no more nuts, no more unworldly prey to take. Many birds had flown away; others had learned to hide or to flee. The turned clods in the empty plots stood sharp and hard in the frost-filled days.

She would go out early, looking for mushrooms, gathering sloes, hips, haws. Gwilym would plod along with her, his hand clasped in hers. His attention would be caught by a cobweb strung with a thousand brilliant jewels of dew, by the golden leaves that clung to the beech trees and rattled in the wind, by a hedgehog snuffling noisily, by a bird that slowly moved along, tossing fallen leaves aside in its hunt for grubs and insects.

The dunnock, a most drab bird, went about slowly and steadily, quite spectacularly unspectacular, a most sober and un-birdlike bird that preferred to plod along the ground rather than to fly.

Perhaps it was its lack of vigour that made it the favourite victim of the irresponsible cuckoo. Could it not feel anger and hurl the intruding chick from the nest? Could it not protect its own chicks? Could it not at least hurl insults at the gods who had made such a bad job of its existence?

Yet perhaps it was conscious of its unjust fate, and conscious of its inability to change that fate. So it sought meekly to make the best of it. Perhaps that was why it would sometimes sing in the night, confiding its pain to the breeze, a song of amazing beauty that filled the blackness for a moment.

The snow started falling that night, thick, dense flakes. The villagers had smelled it all day. By the morning, everything was covered. It was hard to walk through the fields, impossible to catch rabbits and birds. Even foxes and owls were forced to hunt during the day, for they could not catch enough prey in the long winter nights.

Then it froze, day after day, week after week, and the wind blew in from the sea in the west. And the river froze, and the fish were hidden from the villagers, and the birds had fled. Children cried at night. Old people shivered as they tried to gather fallen branches to make a fire.

The widows were always the first to die. Then the sickly children. Then the old. Some said they died of hunger; some said they died of cold. It didn't seem worth arguing about. They were still dead. And the others were still cold and hungry.

Now and again, a weak, silver sun would appear like a shrouded ghost through the drifting sheets of cloud, and, for a couple of minutes, hopes would rise. Then the clouds massed, the light faded, and the icy sleet whipped their thin faces.

Although Gwilym could be counted on to find a glove or to calm a fever, he could do nothing about the snow or the cold. Nor could he prevent the rot that spoiled the food that should have seen them through the darkest days.

The Master exhorted them not to give in, urged them to greater efforts. He was anxious for the day to come when the deal would be final. Often he would ride along the river and look at the mill that would soon be his.

After all, he could not make summer come in winter's place. Yet people still grumbled. People still died.

The Entertainment

On the morning of the wedding, two old women and three children died. An old man, who had gone out to look for wood and for something to eat, was missing. Gwilym found the frozen corpse in the woods.

The Master, anxious for the success of the wedding feast, and although reluctant to pander to the people's superstitions, said he would consult Gwilym.

The guests at the feast were lively -replete with delicious food, enlivened by rich wines- when Gwilym was led in by his mother. Those from further afield had never seen him and were looking forward to this strange spectacle.

Gwilym was dazzled by the hall, and did not know where to look first. Candles and lanterns burned brightly on the tables and in brackets on the walls. Richly coloured tapestries told stories of unicorns and dragons, and of saintly women of impeccable beauty. Light flickered on glasses in which wines of various colours glinted. Pewter platters, glowing fruit, rich costumes, sparkling jewellery -all demanded his attention.

He did not even hear when the Master spoke to him. His mother took his arm, gestured to him that he should pay attention to what the Master was saying. Again, the Master asked what was to be done about the suffering of the people.

Gwilym continued to gaze silently and in wonder at the treasures in the room. The Master was a little annoyed, for he had hoped for better entertainment to bring the feast to a close.

At the far end of the hall, the servants and the villagers, who had, exceptionally, been allowed into the dining-hall, stood in huddled silence. Although they knew it was asking the impossible, they still hoped for the impossible.

"Well?"

Gwilym looked slowly from the tables, at which the Master, his family and his guests were seated, to the villagers by the door, cowed, thin and hungry.

Gwilym moved before his mother could stop him. He went up to the table, picked up an enormous platter and carried it down to the villagers. It could not have been long, but it seemed that he stood there for an age, offering food to those who were too frightened to take it.

The Happiest Man

Gwilym did not know that he had done wrong. Not being blessed with the gift of abstract thought, he did not know that there was such a thing as wrong.

He also did not know that he was being punished. For him, the night tied up in a freezing cellar was just something new.

"A dangerous, meddling fool," the Master decreed.

When he was put in the wagon the next morning, he was excited by the new experiences: the huge horse pulling the wagon, the shine on leather harness coated in frost, the jingling of brasses, the rhythmic, soothing breathing of the horse, the great plumes of mist that shot from its nostrils, the song of a robin keeping a watchful eye to see if any pickings would come its way, the faint smell of the rope in the cold, still morning air.

Standing on the wagon was a new treat; the rope around his neck a new game. He did not even notice his mother crying. He had to be the happiest man ever hanged.

The order was given and the wagon lurched forward. Gwilym no longer laughed. His tongue stuck out in his agonized face, even though, for a few moments, his legs twitched and he flapped his arms, suspended in the air like the dragonfly. Then, like the dragonfly on the water, he stopped moving and hung in silence, limp, motionless. The frost formed in his nostrils.

His mother buried him near the river, for it seemed right to do so. She picked up a handful of frozen earth and threw it down into the hole, saw it scatter across his innocent face.

That evening she sat in the snow by the tree where she used to sit and watch him chase dragonflies. Now her course was run and she was free to go.

* * *

Some live one day; some a thousand years. Yet there is no difference: each moment is full of itself and of nothing else. A fly is born and dies in the time a yew tree, in whose shadow its brief existence is played out, patiently builds another few cells.

As her eyes were closing, she saw a shimmering streak of viridian and patches of cobalt blue as a damselfly settled on a blade of grass. Then it turned and span gently to the river.

In the thick mud, eggs lay. Ugly grey nymphs skulked in this seething sludge. It seemed impossible that they would ever climb up a stem, shed their shells, and dart away on flashing wings of gossamer.

Perhaps we should scream insults at the gods. Perhaps we should throw the cuckoo from the nest. But in the end, the water will weigh down our wings and we will sink.

And if Gwilym lay by the river, it was because, like the dunnock, we cannot change our fate.

Perhaps that is why we, like the dunnock, in the middle of the night, sometimes sing and confide our ills to the breeze.

Lust and the Megalith

A cautionary tale

There are no two ways about it: Llew was a bugger for a megalith.

"You can't beat a megalith. You won't catch me messing about with arches and vaulting and spandrels and bezants and all those other tomfool foreign inventions."

On a fine summer evening, Llew would hold forth on matters historical, cultural and architectural.

The megalith, he would say, had been good enough for his father, and for his father's father, and was good enough for him. The megalith, he would say, had stood the test of time, and, quite pleased with his wit, even somewhat smug, he would direct the gaze of his people to the hills surrounding the village. On the crest of every hill and knoll there were megaliths: single, grouped, in cairns or cromlechs. He would look with a mixture of veneration and proprietorial satisfaction at these stones, some of which marked the boundaries of his lands, some of which marked burial places, most of which marked things lost in the mists of time.

Llew and his people had indeed been there for a long time, for longer than anybody knew. Intruders had come and gone. Strangers had growled from behind the dyke. Yet the megaliths from the start of time defined their lands.

"Don't get me wrong, daub and wattle is fine in its place, and dry stone walling is serviceable enough. But when it comes to something special, when you want to make a bit of a statement, you can't do better than a megalith."

The audience murmured its agreement and pondered the wisdom of their leader.

It was not that he was a stick-in-the-mud, and he had scant time for the old women and dreamers who told stories of magicians and little people. It was just that a megalith showed you were somewhere important, somebody important: a megalith inspired respect.

"And," he added, "with a megalith, once the job is done, it is done."

* * *

Famous last words!

To look at him, you would not think that Llew had ever been in a position to choose between megalith and vaulting shaft. You would not guess that he had been powerful, wealthy, cultured. He skulked around, begging a penny here or there, scrounging an old coat or a pair of worn-out shoes, squabbling with dogs over scraps of food. He talked to himself, gesticulating passionately, and that made the children laugh and tease him.

"Come on, Llew," they taunted, "show us what you're made of."

"Or not," some more worldly-wise urchin added, "as the case may be."

That remark inspired increased hilarity and some quite obscene clutching of groins.

Usually Llew snarled and shuffled away to escape his tormentors. Sometimes he drew himself up, and a flash of anger sparked in his eyes. He had been known to lash out with his stick. The children backed off for a moment, perhaps really frightened, perhaps thinking that the stories about his "little accident" might not be true after all, perhaps just enjoying pretending to be frightened.

But his rage didn't last, and that only made it more fun. They swarmed round, exhilarated by their fear, eager to tame the old beast again, like those who stick swords into a dying bull and mock the flashes of anger in the beast's final agony.

Sometimes he climbed one of the hills above what used to be his land, and sat on the fallen capstone of some ancient cromlech or on the crumbling ruins of those cairns of which he used to be so proud. He looked down on his former domain: the meandering river which, at low tide, left vast expanses of mud flats on which wading birds hunted, but which, at high tide, carried ships right up to the quay in the village. Just above the quay, a long stone bridge crossed the stream and the marshy land alongside, and a hundred yards higher up were the stepping stones and the old church. The fertile valley continued between low hills, dotted with farmhouses, fields and meadows. Between the church and a large house -his former home- there was a cluster of buildings which formed the heart of the village, of the community. Fifty square miles of order, peace and prosperity.

It was not a bad place to be: the soil was fertile, the meadows rich, the area full of wildlife, harmless and nutritious. It rained enough, but not too much. It was neither too hot nor too cold. There was always something to eat, somewhere to shelter, some way of keeping warm. Above all, it was his land. They were his people. There had never been any question about it.

As for the neighbours, on the whole they were good, keeping themselves to themselves in their own place. Now and again there might be some squabble over straying cattle, over a fence which had been moved, over some particularly desirable daughter. At times things got out of hand: alliances would be made, threats issued, age-old arguments restated. Then one party would give or trade a piece of land or a house or a daughter, and things would settle down, with one a little richer, one a little less rich.

* * *

On the whole life was good. If he'd had enough sense to follow his own advice, life would still have been good.

His eyes turned slowly downstream towards the sea. On a low rise by the river sat the intruder in this harmonious landscape, with massive stone walls, incongruous towers and arches.

He had heard enough stories about these immigrants,

but Llew had thought it was all an elaborate joke, a cautionary tale, and everybody enjoyed the idea that the Saxons had been conquered in just one week.

Then the stories told of places this side of the dyke, then of people they had heard of, then of people they knew. They saw neighbours, once wealthy and powerful, cast into poverty and despair, lying in ditches or under bridges, a thin dog curled up at their feet, while the foreigners trampled the land and the people underfoot.

Then his neighbour upstream disappeared, and they moved in, speaking their strange language, throwing their weight around, building mounds and arches and towers and curtain walls, as if the earth had contracted some terrible skin disease.

At first Llew had not been too displeased. He had never got on that well with this particular neighbour, and he hoped that the new owner would be a soft touch, leaving him to collect some pickings along the way.

Llew used to patrol his boundaries, walking the hills, looking down on one side at his own peaceful community, and on the other at the scurrying activity of the newcomers. The men looked such brutes, and he did not know what he would do if, one day, he found them on his land. He prepared barbed comments in his head, polite requests, threats, friendly advice, but he hoped that the situation would never arise.

For the moment, the newcomers were busy building their little castle on top of their mound, apparently as self-satisfied as a dog which finds a tall plant on which to defecate.

* * *

One day, as he was sitting on a ruined cairn, he had been startled by a voice.

"It's just for now, you know, this motte, what you call a little pied-à-terre. Later we will build something much, much better, much, much more big."

Llew was not certain that he fully understood this smoky velvet voice that sighed and moaned with foreign consonants and seductive vowels.

"Oh dear me, I am so silly," she sighed, walking around the cairn and coming into sight, "I startled you. What a silly goose I am!"

She was tall and slim, her figure poorly concealed under a long simple gown of some fine, clinging material. She giggled, put a finger to a pink and pouting lip, peeped from under long, curling eyelashes, and smiled coyly, uncertainly.

"Oh my," she purred, "I hope I have not struck dumb. I am so foolish. When I was so silly as a little girl, my daddy would put me across his knee and spank my little … how do you say?". And she wiggled her little "how-do-you-say" in a most un-little-girl-like manner, and patted it by way of explanation.

It is too easy to be self-righteous now. How should Llew have known of such things? How should he have known that this was naught but a ploy? Llew was not simple, and of course he should have known better. And he did know better -afterwards, too late.

But what red-blooded man confronted with a little "how-do-you-say" has ever known better?

* * *

As the chief in his community, Llew had to see off any challenge, and, like a rutting stag, he spent a lot of time and effort in foolish occupations, making noise, stamping around, locking horns. And, like those of a stag, Llew's couplings were utilitarian and brief, and out of all proportion to the weeks of strutting about and shouting and being a general pain. Llew was not a stranger to sex, but he was a stranger to eroticism, and his dreams that night were troubled by hands slapping young buttocks and by the sultry whisper of "My little how-do-you-say".

"When it is finished," she purred the next day, "it will be so magnifique: high, big, strong, with arches, vaults, spandrels, capitals, pillars, cinquefoils, fillets, dove-tails, arch-stones."

"Sissy stuff," he retorted. "You need some megaliths."

"But the age of the megalith is over," she sighed. "The rounded arch is the future."

"It will never catch on," he said.

"It is progress. Why don't you come down to my place and let me show you my machicolations?" she wheedled, toying with the ends of her wimple.

Not even a saint would have known better.

* * *

The next day, she prattled tantalisingly about buttresses and mantle walls as she led him through the barbican, across the drawbridge, under the deadly spikes of the portcullis. Her witty banter about astragals and parapets was quite bewitching, and when she started on the charms of abutments and groins, Llew's mind wandered down paths which were not at all architectural.

"Voilà," she said, "what do you think?"

She pointed up to the arch above their heads. Llew looked up and saw a series of openings in the stonework, in each of which there was a grinning face. As he looked, one of the faces winked.

"Back to work," she shouted. "You've seen our new neighbour now."

Then she shivered and pulled her gown tight across her body.

"But it is cold out here. Let us go to the sollar. We will be more comfortable for a little chatter."

She led him between walls and towers, under arches, over moats, through a gauntlet of swarthy men busy building, grim smiles creasing their scarred faces.

"One day," she continued, "the arch will be everywhere: pointed arches, barrel arches, ogee arches, curved arches, scalloped arches, mitre arches, horseshoe arches, rampant arches, raised arches, wall arches, relieving arches, trefoil arches."

She paused, moved disturbingly close to Llew, took his hand in hers.

"Why don't you sign up, become my favourite vassal? You could have all this. You would really have one up 'on the Joneses', as I believe you say here."

Llew ap Cadwaladr ap Gwynfeirdd ap Meyric ap

Cynan ap Pwyll ap Man was about to say that he hardly saw himself as the vassal of some jumped up foreigner called Norman, but he decided to hold his tongue.

She led Llew through the outer ward, through the middle ward, and across the inner ward to the much vaunted sollar. She threw open a door and stepped into a room flooded with light from numerous windows set in rounded arches.

"Inside will be the new outside!" she proclaimed. "You can't do that with a megalith. When you have an arch, you can have a window: mullioned, rose, cinquefoils, trefoils."

She turned to Llew alluringly, whispered her little secret.

"You know, I have a soft spot for trefoils."

Llew may not have known what a trefoil was, but he was pretty sure the soft spot she meant was not what he was thinking of.

"Is that another word for ...?" he stuttered.

"You naughty man," she giggled, "is that all you think about? A trefoil is a window with three ..." she hesitated, looked for the words, "trois segments de cercle, three lobes, you know, like a trèfle."

Her hands described curves that sent Llew off on a quite indecent tangent.

"Dim clem," he replied, thinking that two could play that game. "Not the foggiest!"

"Comment? Trèfle," and she reached into her purse. "Trèfle, like in the cards, trefoil, a window with three round things," and she showed Llew a card with a ♣ painted on it.

Llew feigned understanding.

"Perhaps you do not have play cards yet? These were a present from the Bishop of Bamberg himself. Such a nice old man. You see, we have trèfles and coeurs, what you call hearts, and diamonds and …." She showed Llew cards with ♠ on it.

"A spade?" he guessed.

"A spade? Like to dig the ground with?" And she burst out laughing. "How quaint. How very … horticultural. You are so silly. It is a pique, you know, the big thing that you stick in people. Pique!"

"A pike?"

"Voilà. A pike."

"It looks more like a spade to me," Llew grumbled. "Anyway, what can you play with bits of painted paper?"

"The cards are like life itself. Each one has a value. The heart is love, and worth the least. A trèfle, a clover, is better, for it is food, and you can live without love, but not without food. Even better is the diamond which buys both food and love. Best of all is the pike to kill a man and take his money and his food and his love."

"And two is better than one, and three better than two. Then you have the valet who carries out orders, the Queen, who tells the King what orders to give, and then the one who gives the orders, the King."

"Do you want a little game?" she murmured, skilfully

flicking the cards from one hand to the other. "Do you want to play with me?"

"I don't know how," Llew replied.

"It is so easy. I will show you."

She lowered her head, looked up at him from under her eyelids, fluttered her eyelashes.

"It is so warm," she sighed, "Do you mind if I loosen my snood?"

Llew did not know what a snood was, did not know how or how much it might be loosened, but again his mind flew off at another very indecent tangent.

"It is so easy," she purred persuasively. "We each take two cards, we show one of them and whoever shows the highest card wins."

She picked up the cards, put two in front of Llew and took two herself.

Llew had the ten of trèfles. She turned over the ten of hearts.

"You win," she called out excitedly, "your trèfle beats my heart. It is the beginner's luck. Now you choose."

Llew picked two cards. He turned over the Queen of Hearts. She picked two and turned over the nine of diamonds.

"You win again," she pouted, "I think you are taking advantage of a young girl, pretending that you have not played before. That is very, very naughty."

Llew could have protested that the game was not quite as challenging as the rules of *cynghanedd*, but he was busy thinking of how to take advantage of his very fetching, but rather dim new neighbour.

Again and again she sulked and pouted and stamped her little foot and sighed and complained that Llew was very naughty.

"It is good we aren't playing for money," she said.

"I haven't got any money," Llew lied with the peasant's instinctive reaction.

"Or even worse." A faint blush suffused her cheeks with a rosy bloom of innocence. "Some people play for their ..., and then I would be ...."

Her hands reckoned quickly what she was wearing, passed lightly from gown to belt to wimple to snood, and then made mysterious calculations of what might lie beneath.

Llew quickly counted up his own clothing, pleased that, like any good peasant, he never cast a clout no matter what month was out.

"Oh dear," she groaned, "completely ...."

Llew imagined the rustle of silk slipping from her, saw her try to cover herself with her hands, heard her sigh in his ear.

"Thank goodness for these rounded arches, or I would catch my death of colds."

"Perhaps you might fancy a ...," and she peeped out from under her lashes, "... a little flutter. It's just silliness."

Llew dithered.

"But we would stop before ...," and her gestures called up a vision of her indefensible nudity.

"Besides," she added, "it would not be fair. You have so many clothings, and I have just .... You see, in here there is no draughts, and you don't need …."

She gestured vaguely at Llew's attire.

"So perhaps it is not interesting for you," she murmured, "I do not have much to play with."

"Not that we have to play at all," she concluded. "I have so much more interesting things to tell you about trefoils."

"All right," he stammered.

"All right what?" she urged.

"All right. I'll play," he croaked.

She turned aside, raised her hands as if to hide what the chemise soon wouldn't.

"For our clothings?"

"Yes," whispered Llew.

"But we stop before …. We don't play for everything, do we?"

"Everything," stammered Llew.

"Everything?" she questioned with wide-eyed apprehension.

"Everything," he stuttered.

"Just our clothings. Not …, you know, not …, not for everything?" she asked.

"Everything," Llew blurted out.

"Goods and chattels? Body and soul?"

"Yes," croaked Llew.

"You are so naughty," she demurred, "I do not think I should be playing such a game with a man like you.

My daddy would be putting me across his knee if he knew."

* * *

They sat down at opposite sides of a small table which she appeared to conjure out of thin air.

She took two cards and turned over the seven of spades. Llew turned over the Jack of hearts. Her previously loosened snood fell to the ground.

She took two cards and turned over the six of diamonds. Llew turned over the Queen of clubs. She slowly removed her wimple, letting long silken tresses fall about her shoulders.

She reached over and squeezed Llew's hand. "You are so very bad. You are winning all the time," she said. "Will you give me a chance, let me take an extra card?"

Llew looked at her suspiciously.

"Or course, for an extra card I double my stake, so if I lose I have to take off two things."

Llew's heart rate and his expectations rose.

"And if I take two extra, I take off ...." She silently made an inventory of her garments that left Llew gasping.

"We can take extra cards," Llew conceded magnanimously.

"Will you choose first?" she asked.

Five of clubs and the two of hearts. She chose her cards. He was the first to take an extra card and picked the nine of spades.

"Jack of Spades," she called out gaily. "Two clothings, please!"

Llew removed his gloves, quite happy to feel air somewhere on his body.

She chose her cards. He picked the three of hearts and the Queen of spades. He prayed silently for her to take an extra card. She did. She still looked uncertain.

"Oh dear," she groaned, "I can no more take cards, for if I lose I will be …. I have only three things left."

"Queen of Spades," Llew croaked.

"Oh dear," she whispered.

She let her belt and gown slip from her shoulders.

"You are a naughty man," she giggled. "You must not be peeping."

Drops of sweat ran down his face. He thought that he heard somebody laugh, and he looked around, but nobody was there. It was hard to concentrate, for the scrap of modesty afforded by her decorative rather than protective chemise was inflammatory.

He picked the Jack of diamonds and the two of clubs. He picked an extra card, the two of spades. He picked again: the ten of hearts.

She hesitated and then took a third card and then a fourth.

"It is the all or nothing," she smiled.

He turned over the Jack.

She turned over the King of Spades.

He definitely did hear a chortle. He span round and saw faces peeping through the windows.

"Who are they?" he demanded.

"Nobody really. Go away," she called out, "I am with our new neighbour."

It was a relief to remove his hat, coat, scarf and jacket.

He got the Jack of Spades and the nine of hearts. He grinned across the table. She had the King of Spades.

A door opened, and those who had been at the windows hurried in, their faces contorted with laughter.

Llew stood up angrily and removed his shirt. He tried to remember how many holes he had in his more intimate garments.

He took an extra card, lost again. He swore, and took off his boots.

He took an extra card.

"Queen of Clubs," he snapped.

She had the King of Spades.

She laughed. He complained. The crowd booed. Some large, rough looking men came and stood quite close to him. He took off his leggings.

He dealt. He changed twice. She had the King of Spades.

He argued. She smiled. A very large man came and stood beside her. Llew recognised the face that had winked at him earlier.

He took off shirt and socks. He was down to three items. Almost even.

The spectators roared their approval. Some chanted.

She dealt. She had the King of Spades.

He protested and complained. She coaxed and soothed. His vest and trousers joined the mound of clothing on the floor. The crowd whistled and cheered at his long, shapeless underwear. Llew sat down sullenly.

He dealt. He picked up the King of Diamonds and the King of Spades! At last! He laughed out loud, stood up, shouted at the hostile spectators, made rather rude gestures.

He felt conspicuous in his long underwear and sat down, and to belie any impression he might have given that he had good cards, he took another two, hoping she would do the same.

She smiled uncertainly, hesitated, took an extra card. Two items, he thought, her chemise and her. He composed the start of a poem, in strict meter, praising his courage for having stayed and seen it through. Then, O! joy of joys, she changed again.

He threw down the King of Spades triumphantly.

She turned over the King of Spades.

The crowd convulsed with laughter. He stared at the two Kings.

"Cheat" he shouted.

The crowd grumbled. She protested her innocence.

"I never said there was only one King," she said gently.

Why had he gone lusting in the first place? Why couldn't he have been content with his own little farm? Then he remembered that he also had the King of Diamonds and a crafty glint came into his eye.

"The second card should decide," he suggested nonchalantly. She agreed.

Llew turned over the King of Diamonds and punched the air.

She turned over the King of Spades.

"And I never said there were only two," she chortled.

The crowd was ecstatic. Voices chanted and sang. "Four. Four. We want four," they clamoured.

"I think you have lost," she said quietly.

Llew was furious. He ripped off his underwear. The crowd jeered at his sadly deflated manhood. He stood naked for a moment and then turned to leave with as much dignity as he could muster.

"Four. Four. We want four. Four. Four. Still three more," the crowd howled.

"We did say we were playing for everything, didn't we?" she asked quietly, like a patient but unrelenting schoolmistress. "If I am not mistaken, you do still owe three items."

She beckoned him to the table on which she placed several sheets of paper and a pen.

Llew had to sign away everything he possessed.

He turned, forcing himself up straight to walk naked, but with dignity, through the caterwauling crowd. Now he understood his neighbours.

"Four. Four. Still two more," they screamed.

Llew summoned the last shreds of his pride.

"I have nothing more to give you."

She smiled.

"I think you do. Not much," she said, playing shamelessly to the crowd, "not much, but ...." She took a knife from the man standing by her, pulled a hair from her head, held it between forefinger and thumb of the left hand and sliced it in two with a flick of a knife.

The crowd exploded with laughter.

His hands fell to protect himself.

"Body and soul," she smiled. She looked down at her prizes. "Well, not exactly a pound of flesh," she called to the crowd. The crowd chanted without restraint.

"And now, my friend," and she approached slowly, "tu as été couillonné et maintenant tu seras découillonné! The would-be screwer is screwed. You played and you lost. Everything!"

By that very evening, the foreigners had moved into his house. Later they started to build a little mound further downstream, and soon there were arches and towers everywhere. The future had indeed arrived.

* * *

Llew hangs around, hiding in pigsties and huts, scrounging a coin here and there, talking to himself with words no-one understands, taunted by the children and chased by dogs. Now and again, he draws himself up straight, turns on his tormentors, but usually he doesn't bother, can no longer remember the days of the megalith.

✤ ✤ ✤

A Very Boring Day

A rather dark moral story

The sport had not been good at all. The lawn that stretched away down the hill in front of them may well have been dotted with red patches, but that was not enough. It had been too easy. The birds had flown straight; the game had run half-heartedly, apparently too lethargic even to try to save its life. Even the tricks had not worked. Charles had let a hare get almost right across the lawn to within a few yards of the trees, but even then, when he had taken a shot, there had been just another puff of red. They had tried to get a rabbit going by shooting in front of it, causing great spurts of earth to be thrown up, halting the animal, turning it round in its tracks. It had crossed the lawns twice, but just as they were becoming interested, it had sat down and waited, bewildered. Thomas had been so disgusted that he had put in one of his special cartridges. The rabbit simply disappeared in a spurt of gore and soil.

"Next," James had cried out.

A pigeon had flapped from the trees forty yards away.

He had fired and the fat body had dropped to the ground.

The killing had been too easy, too routine. They had not been able to sustain an erection at all. The girls were bored and frustrated, and made no bones about letting it be known. They lounged distractedly, and made comments about the peasants, those men who were coming and going from the buildings down into the trees with the birds and animals for the kill, and who went about their business as quickly and as inconspicuously as possible, trying not to attract the attention of the group on the terrace, trying not to hear the suggestions of the young women, or to see what they were doing.

"Next."

A woodcock was pitched from the trees. It hesitated and then darted low across the grass, swerved into the evening sun. Thomas fired, and cursed. His companions laughed and the girls glanced around. The bird dashed for the cover of the trees but was driven back by the waiting peasants with their noise machines. It swooped and veered and headed to the terrace. Henry swung around, fired. The bird twisted, and flew away down the lawn. There was a burst of applause, and then the hideous noise of guns. The bird shuddered, zigzagged towards the trees again. There was another deafening salvo, and twigs and leaves were ripped from the trees. Yet the bird flew on. Soon it would be out of range.

Thomas lifted his gun again, took aim carefully. He was excited at last. He fired. The bird drooped, flapped one wing stubbornly, and then spiralled to the earth. It struggled valiantly, hauling the tatters of its body across the grass. Those far off on the terrace applauded.

"It's mine," Thomas shouted.

The girls clustered around him, their eyes fixed on the tiny scrap dragging itself fitfully across the grass. He turned and studied the excited faces. Which one would he take? And how? His excitement mounted. He reached into his pocket, brought out a special cartridge. He held it out to Jane. Her eyes glinted and she nodded. Perhaps now, straight away, in front of them all. After all, he was the only one to manage it so far that day.

He turned back to the lawn where the bird still struggled weakly. He loaded the cartridge and snapped the gun closed. Each moment lasted deliciously as he lifted the gun, breathed in, braced himself. He heard the sharp intake of breath from those around him, could smell the girls pressing against him.

"What's that?" someone called out.

A small boy ran across the grass, heading for the dying woodcock. He scooped it up, cupped it in his hands and headed back for the trees.

"Well," shrieked Charles, "let's teach the brat a lesson."

He swung his gun to his shoulder, aimed carefully. The earth ten yards in front of the boy was ripped up. The child faltered, turned to the terrace, and then raced on again. Charles was not amused. He fired again. Five yards in front of the boy. Priscilla tittered and clapped. The others lifted their guns and fired. The boy choked, stumbled, blinded by the curtain of soil. Confused, he raced back across the clearing.

The woodcock slipped from his hands and writhed on the ground.

"It's mine," Thomas said, and fired.

* * *

On the whole, the funeral had been quite a success. The boy's mother looked out through her grief, and through the veil of her new hat, and saw the shining carriages and the gleaming coffin. The brothers and sisters were so afraid of spoiling their new clothes that they hesitated to walk right to the edge of the small grave. The father, unused to alcohol, saw little, was not at times certain which child it was that had been lost.

The Friends from the House had not been able to go themselves, of course, but they had sent a secretary in a grey suit. He stood impassively throughout the service, kissed the hand of the mother afterwards, and then disappeared without a word.

The lawyers had worked very hard and had come to an agreement. There was no question about the fact that it had been an accident, a most unfortunate accident. That was understood. However, the Friends had paid for the funeral and for all the necessary, if trivial details -decent clothes for the family, food and drink as required, the refurbishing of the cottage so that the coffin could be displayed to the neighbours in adequate surroundings, even, much to the misplaced joy of the children, the loan of a bath sent down from the House so that the family could be clean on this occasion. All these details had been attended to.

Moreover, a certain sum had been left with the parents, in case of any future and unforeseen expenses, the lawyers had explained. The parents had studied the papers with numb disbelief.

The lawyers had presented their report to those at the House.

Priscilla had read through the accounts, had burst out laughing.

"Is that all you paid for the mother's dress?" she questioned. "She must have looked simply awful."

And she sent for the secretary in the grey suit that very instant to have her opinion confirmed.

And they had all agreed that the lawyers had done their work well, that, in the end, when all was said and done, the whole thing had cost less than a decent day's fishing.

* * *

To escape the tedium that fell upon the House, they decided to go away. The tour would be the thing to revive them, they concluded, to give them back their joie de vivre.

In the cottages, the neighbours huddled and gossiped. They knew each button of each item of clothing that had been given. They knew each bottle of beer that had been drunk, each morsel of food that had been eaten, and those that had been hidden away for another day.

Of course, it was terrible to lose a child like that. But then, children do die anyway. There was not a family in the village that had not lost a child at some time. But those children had been packed in a crate and hastily consigned to the earth. Life was too hard to mourn too extravagantly.

The mother mourned her child in silence, weeping in the hostile hour of dawn. The money would be used for a monument to her child, and to the cruelty of the world in general, and of those at the House in particular. Not a penny would be used otherwise. A monument of love and hatred.

In the cottages, the neighbours watched.

The sick child that died that week was hastily buried. There were no new clothes or carpets, no new bed, no bath, no man in a grey suit to kiss the hand of the grieving mother. The parents of the child that had been shot had sent a wreath: one left over, some said; just a cheap one, others said; and with them all living in luxury just because their simple-minded son had wanted to save some bird.

The sickly felt the unspoken reproach that their death would be futile, unprofitable.

The mother of the boy who had been shot mourned her child in her new bed, and now and again smiled wistfully at this unfamiliar self in the mirror so richly turned out in mourning clothes.

* * *

They returned to the House on a Friday evening. The building that had lain still for months echoed with shrill laughter and loud voices. They clattered up the staircases, bounced on the beds. The tour had been very exciting, but it was quite heady to be back. They called to each other in odd words of foreign languages, and the House echoed with their noises until late into the night, until satiation and fatigue stilled them.

For a few days, life was hectic. They raged through the grounds, bathed naked in the lakes, chastised the peasants on any pretext, and then laughed hilariously. Visits were made and received, and life recaptured its sparkle.

But it palled slowly. Their frenzy subsided. Their appetites could not be revived. They bickered. Even their most complicated sensual experiments became familiar, and their imaginings could go no farther. Visits were boring, the lake too cold, and the peasants were so stupid and so obsequious that it was no fun goading them.

The birds again flew straight. The game ran feebly across the clearing. The bloody piles littering the lawns were not exciting. Now and again they got some amusement from an injured animal that struggled quite ridiculously to drag away what remained of its body, or that performed strange contortions in its agony. But even this was neither interesting nor amusing for long. Thomas would insert the special cartridges and put an end to it.

They had been shooting, and failing to fornicate, for over thirty minutes when, just as Thomas was going to finish a fine partridge that was struggling on the ground, a child emerged from the trees on the right. The Friends called out, and Thomas lowered his gun. A second accident would be tedious, without even the thrill of novelty.

"Come back. Come back and keep low!" the peasants shouted from the trees. They glanced up at the terrace where they were angrily gesticulating. The child stood in the middle of the clearing, waving the bleeding body over his head.

"Come back," his mother cried, and she almost ran out into the clearing.

The child did not answer. The blood of the bird ran down his waving, upstretched arm. Tears ran down his frightened face. He stared at the terrace, willing them to shoot. He uttered every curse he knew, every word he should not have known, hated with the intense and despairing impotence of a child. He heard his mother call, the voice that was slowly cracking and breaking under the weight of life.

"Shoot."

He saw his mother, beautiful in black, his sisters playing with new dolls, his father ..., well, perhaps drunk in the street.

"Shoot."

"Little swine," James shouted. "Clear off."

"Quite spoilt it all," Charles complained.

"His father is finished here," Thomas promised.

"And they're so ugly," Jane sighed.

"Come back," the mother implored.

Her son, her best son. Blasted and torn. She saw the ripped body, the glistening coffin, the tall man in grey who stood silently and who came and kissed her hand.

Those on the terrace had tired of waving and cursing and they leaned indecisively against the parapet.

A blush of shame came to the child's face, but he had

to make them shoot. He dropped the limp body of the partridge and pulled off his clothes. He turned his back to the terrace and bent down. Between his legs, he saw the reaction, saw them gather at the parapet in consternation. He straightened up, turned to the House, and began to dance across the grass, making gestures as obscene as he knew how. He saw them arguing on the terrace, saw a gun glint, heard a shot, and then saw the leaves ripped from the trees to his left. He turned and bent over and then danced away in the other direction. Tears ran down his blushing face as he danced naked with the shots whistling over him, to one side of him and then to the other. Then he heard his mother scream.

* * *

On the terrace they copulated magnificently. They were not sure whose shot it had been that had finally dropped the boy, but it did not matter, for they had all shared the excitement, and they coupled fiercely and promiscuously until the chill of the night drove them indoors.

The secretary had spoken to the peasants and called the lawyers. It was both more difficult and yet easier this time. Of course, a second accident was deplorable, and they were quite overcome at the House. But then again, the child had had no reason to run across the firing area, and then to seem unable, unwilling even, to get away. It was as if it had been intentional, the lawyers had suggested. The peasants had protested. They should not have fired. They could see there was a child. And not a simpleton either. Not like the previous one. A good boy, the best son, the hope of the family who could already earn a man's wage.

And the price for a best son who could earn a man's wage was agreed.

The lawyers went away to report to the House.

"Is that all?" they hooted, and coupled with renewed vigour.

The funeral took place amidst beer and new clothes, and the man in grey did kiss the mother's hand and leave without a word. And the family did grow strong and healthy, with better food and clothes, although nothing could replace the best son, as the mothers of the two dead children, the simpleton and the best son, agreed over tea, and the fathers agreed over a pipe of good tobacco in the evening.

And the neighbours watched and waited.

Winter came, and food was scarce, and another accident took place. A very good one, they all agreed at the House. An older boy, quite mature, as the girls added eagerly and somewhat to the chagrin of the men, running naked in the afternoon, dodging, zigzagging, dropping suddenly and then racing away again. They had missed time and time again, even though they had been trying this time. James had finally clipped him, and Thomas had finished him.

They had celebrated throughout the night. The lawyers and the parents negotiated and argued and finally agreed.

And three mothers grieved over tea and cakes, and three fathers puffed at their pipes.

Parents began to look at their children in a different way. Not that any parent would wish the death of even one child, even though they had so many that they could not feed them all properly, even though they had so many that they did not know immediately just how many, but would have to stop and count on their stubby, dirty fingers, and even though any peasant knows that a certain pruning was always good for the plant. No, nobody could wish for such a terrible thing.

But accidents do happen. People fall ill, and one can never tell in this life. And it's a shame to waste things, especially when you have so little.

Children felt the unspoken pressure. Some succumbed, and ran, and were buried with great pomp. Their parents grieved and keened over linen cloths and tea and cake. The cemetery filled with tiny graves. It seemed that only those families without children, or those who had children of unusual selfishness, remained in poverty. It seemed that they brought it on themselves.

At the House they had difficulty finding enough peasants to do all the work, for the newly-rich villagers now disdained the humbler jobs. So peasants were brought in from other villages, and the native peasants grouped together to make sure that the children of these outsiders did not try to have an accident.

In the village, late at night, the peasants feverishly tried to make replacements for the children they had lost. In the early mornings, they lay awake making intricate calculations.

The Friends at the House tried to learn restraint. Stock management. But once a week, they went out to shoot rabbits and hares and snipe. Ostensibly.

"Next," called Charles, and a pheasant whirred briefly.

"Next," called James, and a rabbit ran and fell.

"Next," called Thomas, and a pigeon disintegrated.

"Next," called Joseph.

The excitement screamed through their minds and bodies as a small, white form swayed from the trees. As true sportsmen they took turns, and grumbled when they missed. Some of the children were very good. Some lasted for ages, dodging and weaving, dropping to their knees and then suddenly sprinting. It was sometimes almost a shame.

A rate had been worked out by the peasants and the lawyers. Each extra second of life could be monetized. Each feint and bob could ensure the well-being of the survivors. Both the peasants and the lawyers had their own timekeepers. The calls from the families hiding in the trees changed. The despairing pleas to the child to come back gave way to screams of encouragement to last a little longer, to keep going, to think of the family. The death sentence had been pronounced already, and it was only the price that remained to be settled.

Some were weak.

"An insult, really," Thomas maintained, and fired.

They all agreed that they wouldn't pay for that one.

"Next," he called despondently.

* * *

A youth walked calmly from the trees. He was tall and slim. His body was taut and muscular. He came to the middle of the clearing, turned to face the terrace, raised his arms over his head, his hands clasped, confronted them with his nakedness.

On the terrace they called to one another, a little nonplussed. The girls stared, tittered, and pointed out the obvious to each other in loud whispers. The men were, for some strange reason, somewhat embarrassed.

The youth lowered his arms. He bowed to the group up on the terrace, and then he ran. Before the men had even reacted, he had got clean across the lawn to the trees where he disappeared.

The girls giggled, and the men grumbled that they hadn't been ready. After all, this was new. They waited quietly, wondering what would happen next. Suddenly the youth reappeared ten yards closer to them. He darted in a low crouch towards the House, and, just before the first shots whistled around him, he turned and raced straight across the lawn heading for the trees. They hurriedly aimed and fired, but he had turned, and was now zigzagging towards them. Before they could reload, he was safe in the trees. The sound of applause came from the trees up to the House.

Again he dashed from the trees, this time forty yards further away, just on the rise of the land. He raced, and then dropped to the ground in a fold of the land, just in time as the shots rang out. He lay for some seconds, and then he headed back up towards the House again, racing for another hollow.

The peasants cheered enthusiastically, consulted their new watches and congratulated the family of this intrepid runner. On the terrace, the girls clapped their hands and danced. The men were rather surly, and hastily tried to come to some agreement about a firing order for the next appearance of the boy.

Again, he spurted from his shelter, weaved and dodged, and reached the trees. Blood ran from his side where he had been grazed. He stared at the wound in disbelief, for he felt no pain, and yet his flesh was ripped open. He felt only a wild exhilaration, an intensity of existence. He darted out onto the lawn again, waving his hands at the group on the terrace, racing cunningly from one fold in the land to another, crawling a few yards unseen, and then racing out again. Soon he was back in the trees, surrounded by the peasants and his family.

They stared at the hole in his side.

"That's enough," his mother wept. And she tried to wrap her shawl around his wounds and his nakedness.

And the peasants agreed, perhaps a little reluctantly, for this was the record, and he would have earned a fortune.

He drew his mother's shawl around his body, and leapt shouting from the trees. He ran like a madman, jumping and dancing, weaving and dodging, startling the group so much that he had got to the other side almost before they had realised. The guns all fired at the same moment, and the tree behind which he had dashed was torn by the shots. The shawl was soaked in blood and hung heavily around him. He edged carefully up through the trees until he was only some forty yards from the Terrace. His excitement had been replaced by weariness, his joy by a pervasive awareness of futility. It had to be, and this was the time.

He summoned his last energies and raced for the centre of the lawn, so close to the terrace that he could hear the men grunt, that he could hear the sharp intake of the girls' breath. The shots rang out as he collapsed into the hollow. He felt the wound now. It was so unbearably intense he could not tell whether it was pain or pleasure.

If he didn't get up soon, he realised, he would not be able to get up at all, and that was not the way he wanted to go: there was no defiance in lying in a hole in the middle of the lawn, letting your life drip away. He dragged himself to his feet, and stared at the House. As he rose, twelve guns swung round at him. They wavered when he did not run.

"He's done for, the bastard," Thomas laughed. "We've got him now."

And he raised his gun slowly, peered down the barrel at the shape in front of him, a naked body draped in a dripping shawl. His finger eased on the trigger. Around him there was silence. The group said nothing. They even seemed not to breathe. In the trees, the peasants had fallen silent. Some had even edged out from the trees to witness the event.

Thomas released the trigger and lowered his gun.

The girls threw themselves at their companions. They writhed feverishly in each other's arms until late into the evening. Even then, they slept fitfully, waking now and again to embrace whichever body lay nearby.

The youth had slipped to the ground, despairing, and losing consciousness as he had watched Thomas lower his gun and turn away. He had been carried home to the village, to the poor hut in which his family lived. And would now continue to live, thought the others, for the Friends had refused to shoot.

His wounds had been cleaned and dressed, but for many days he had lain between life and death.

* * *

The lawyers had come, and had paid anyway. Those whose children had died thought that that was quite unfair. They had even paid extra, a bonus from the young ladies, the lawyers had explained impassively.

For quite some time, Thomas had sulked, maintaining that it was not fair because they had not been expecting such a performance, had not known what to do. He was really quite jealous of his reputation as a shot. The others had ragged him, and slowly he came to see their point, to laugh at himself, to admit that it was better that way.

However, he still maintained, it would have been better if they had known what was going on, what the rules were. And, over wine and brandy, they made up rules. They sought by ever finer legislation to balance the runner between life and death. As they argued and pontificated, they all kept in mind the sight of that naked youth standing on the lawn, draped in a blood-sodden rag.

It was only because he was uncertain as to what to do on a cool and cloudy afternoon that William suggested a shoot at all. They called the men and went out onto the terrace. Birds and rabbits and even one or two deer fell to their casual shots and they all applauded each other politely. One or two of the girls took turns, and were generally thought to have performed quite well. By five o'clock they went into the House to change.

The next morning was bright and sunny, but nobody went out. They hung about idly. Rodney was reading. Mary had dragged out her box of water-colours, and daubed endless sheets of paper with meaningless smears. David sent servants looking for every pencil in the House, and he then sharpened them all. Jane had all the new kittens brought to her, and she drowned them in a large wooden bucket. Her hands were covered in scratches that evening.

Three children of those peasants who had been brought in to do the lowest jobs died that week. It was so cold that they could not dig proper graves, and the bodies had to be kept in a shed. The other peasants thought that that was not very nice. There was nothing they could do about it, but they withdrew even further from any contact with the new poor of the estate.

Then one of their children, the brother of one who had already died, one who had already "given", as they called it between themselves, fell through the ice on the lake and drowned. In the village, the peasants grumbled about how stupid it was to die like that, without charge, as it were. Some said they thought the House should pay for the child anyway, even though they could not say why, and there were quite some rumblings of discontent about this wasted death. A spokesman asked the lawyers to call so that they could put their case. The lawyers came down to the village, but dismissed their pretensions. Many of the peasants grumbled, for, as they demanded of the lawyers, how were they expected to live? The lawyers demurred. You got paid if you went according to the rules, they maintained.

*   *   *

Two days later, the villagers sent word to the House that they would like a run as soon as was convenient.

The secretary in the grey suit was made responsible for etiquette, and for the observance of the newly elaborated Rules.

They prepared with great earnest, for what had been no more than an idle pastime was now invested with a ritual significance. They dressed and groomed themselves very carefully, and the girls wore the evening gowns that they had worn for the reception in Vienna, and which had caused such a stir even there. At the correct time, they filed down to the Terrace in formal procession and took up their places.

They were to stand five yards back from the parapet against which the guns had been positioned. The runner was to walk, naked, from the trees to the centre of the lawn where he would turn and salute the group. The secretary would give the signal to commence and the sport would begin. While the sportsmen rushed for their guns, the runner would have a chance to get back to the cover of the trees.

But this runner didn't even move. He was simply ripped apart by the first shots, and where was the sport in that?

They had been cheated.

They went into the House absolutely fuming. They called for the secretary to come at once. The rules had to be changed, they complained.

"Right," shouted Charles. "If the bastard cannot even get past the opening move, cannot even get to the trees to start with, then they do not get paid at all."

They all agreed. Some even wanted to penalise the peasants, but, as Jane pointed out, they had nothing that was worth the bother of taking. Except on the run itself, of course.

The displeasure of the group was conveyed to the peasants in no uncertain manner by the lawyers. Such devious goings-on were not at all sporting, they admonished, and would not be tolerated.

Subsequent runs were more successful. As they gained more experience, they tinkered with the rules, ever refining them to obtain even more exquisite pleasure, to more finely balance life and death.

Each run became more like life itself, with its chances, its successes, with its pain and failures, and with the eternal, if naive, hope that the inevitable would be avoided.

It was so much like life that, in the end, it became more painful to try to avoid death than to give oneself up to it, and it would be difficult to say whether it was more of a pleasure to the group to dispense death than it was to the runner to receive it.

* * *

In the autumn, word was brought to the House that the youth was prepared to run again.

The days were drawing in quickly and it was cold and overcast on the afternoon of the run. They huddled in their tweeds and leathers in the grey drizzle as they waited on the terrace. The girls wrapped their capes tight around themselves and shivered from the cold and from excitement. Down in the woods, they could hear the bustle of the peasants, for all the villagers had come to see their hero run, and they chattered unrestrainedly among themselves -something they would never have dared to do before. The group were displeased by this behaviour, and they promised themselves that they would reaffirm the customary discipline amongst the peasants. The peasants even showed themselves among the trees, and Thomas wanted to let off one or two warning shots into the branches. The peasants even dared cheer when the secretary finally gave the signal and the youth strode haughtily out onto the grass.

The girls stared and giggled. They were not disappointed. Cynthia even applauded, but the glances from the men soon called her to herself.

The youth stood in the starting position, turned to the terrace and saluted. He stood absolutely still while the secretary checked that all was as it should be. When the signal was given, the runner was presumptuous enough to bow to the group as they started to move for their guns. He waited for what seemed an impossibly long time before turning and racing for cover. The explosions rang out in the heavy air just as he slid behind a great oak.

He had a gift of slipping unseen between the trees and bushes, of reappearing quite unexpectedly for his next dash. He could run and swerve so quickly that their shots always missed. His pace and direction were so unpredictable that he foiled them time after time.

As twilight fell, the smoke from the guns hung heavily over the terrace. The secretary stepped out and raised his arm: the run was over. The men were tired, but the girls were so inordinately excited that they could not, and did not contain themselves. Their wildness soon revived the spirits of the men as they recalled the frail, spectral body that had weaved miraculously among storms of lead, had saluted and jutted shamelessly at them.

Good as some of the others were, they did appear as something of an anticlimax. Some were very fast and agile, and some completed several dashes before being caught. But they were all caught, and somehow the moment when they suddenly halted their insane race, spun and fell in a spurt of blood was less satisfying, less exhilarating than it should have been.

"Next," they called abruptly, almost peevishly, always hoping that their appetites could be sharpened, their senses teased to satisfaction.

And "Next" again when another pale body was borne away.

They had had enquiries made. The runner lived now in a large cottage on the edge of the village, and was renowned both because of the money he had earned, and because of the way he was spending it. His house echoed throughout the nights with laughter and cries. The cooks and merchants of the villages came to the cottage laden with goods. It was reported, the lawyers said, lowering their voices and looking round as if they feared being caught repeating such things, that he had been offered most of the girls of the village, and had taken them all. The girls listened to these reports with lustful curiosity; the men with envy.

It became a habit, when they went for a canter across

the estate, to turn down through the forest towards the settlements, and to skirt the village. Through the trees they saw the cottage set back from the lane. Sometimes they saw somebody going in, and, once, a young girl skipping away. They never saw the runner. Once they heard a terrible shout, and they wondered if it was him, but they could not be sure.

The runner's appetites grew daily and were the wonder of the peasants.

Although she was the quietest, and apparently the most discreet, Margaret was the one who finally could not resist the temptation. She had gone out for a walk, so she had told the others and herself, repeating the story she had so long rehearsed. She had broken her shoe and had knocked at the first cottage to send to the house for help.

She had gone back and forth several times before she finally went up to the door and knocked. The door had opened and he had stood there. Naked. Absolutely naked.

"I ...," she had stammered.

He laughed, and stood back from the door.

She stared again and then simply walked in, not even bothering with her story of a broken shoe.

He had not said a word, and she had calmly set about inspecting the cottage. At each door she stopped, and he opened it, and she went inside. Without a word. She saw a sitting room, a rough kitchen and a room at the back that was absolutely empty. Then she went upstairs. A door was opened, and she went in to find the fabled bed and perhaps a dozen naked girls lounging on it. She turned to the runner, but his face remained impassive. She left the room and hesitated. But there was no point. She had come this far and had no pride to lose in front of a peasant, and so she continued her tour. The other rooms were all empty. Then she went downstairs and to the front door that still stood open.

"I broke my shoe," she stated haughtily and flounced away.

The runner said nothing, He stood in the doorway until she turned to look back when she got to the road. He laughed, and she turned away quickly and strode off.

The following week they all went shooting again. The runners were not bad, really, but the reactions of the group had become much faster and they could guess changes in speed and direction with great skill. Even those the peasants counted on most could scarcely survive more than one or two dashes.

There was also a certain desire for revenge born of envy which found its expression in the speed with which they dropped the runners.

The peasants complained, for nobody could last for long, and the price was low. And stocks were not inexhaustible. They argued about the rules, saying that they were unfair, but the lawyers merely mentioned the runner and left. Some of the least thrifty peasants had to ask for their jobs back. Others went to see the priest, and prayed for the Word to be realised.

But the peasants still sent their young to run, and they buried them, resentful that they had not run faster, lasted longer.

The Friends shot and killed and copulated.

"Next," they called. They wanted to get one on the first dash, but they hadn't managed that yet.

The priest had spoken against the runner, had pronounced a curse on him. The runner had laughed when he had been told, and had not even bothered to open the door when the priest had come with his attendants to visit the cottage and to encircle it. Even as they repeated the terrible words, so the lawyers said, they had heard screams of pleasure coming from the upstairs room. The peasants had not dared to contradict the priest, but they still sent their daughters to the runner.

He sent word that he would run again in the spring.

Great preparations were made, both in the House and in the villages. Feasts and banquets were planned. Even those living in most misery looked forward to the great day. Or, perhaps, especially those living in misery dreamed of the day. The Secretary reported that the peasants were working less than they should, that they were becoming touchy and sometimes almost insolent.

It would be dealt with after the run, Charles retorted and dismissed him.

* * *

The runner survived yet again, and was borne back to the village on the shoulders of the peasants.

Thomas could scarcely believe that they had not managed to drop him. Perhaps the terrible things that the Priest claimed were right. It had to be investigated.

The pretext could be the rules, James suggested.

Priscilla leapt from her chair, raced over and kissed him.

"That's it," she cried. "The rules. Tell him we must see him to discuss the rules."

Word was sent by the Secretary that he was to come to the House.

The word was known throughout the village in minutes. No peasant had ever gone to the House other than as a worker. No good could come of this, said some. It's the curse, others muttered. Some went to tell the priest.

The runner said nothing, and did nothing to change his ways. On the day appointed, he walked up to the House, watched by the peasants hiding in the woods.

They had to consider the rules, Charles started.

They had considered that it would be more sporting to modify certain points, he continued. They outlined various proposals, argued the merits of certain suggestions, discussed at length the true nature of sport and of gentlemen.

"No," the runner said.

The girls stepped back in surprise. They had been examining him and discussing him among themselves with little more restraint than they would use when discussing a horse. They had carefully appraised his body, while the men had attempted to engage his mind with the subtleties of the rules.

"No," he said. Then he turned and left.

The peasants asked a hundred questions and every answer was repeated from mouth to mouth. They now held the runner in awe and they withdrew the intimacy of equality from him.

The priest did not come to meet him on his return.

The Friends sent for him again. He came late in the evening, when the warmth of the day was fading. He was reddened by the sun, his hair bleached.

The girls lounged in their chairs and peered up at him in the gathering twilight. They had no intention of being abandoned so hastily this time.

The men flattered and the girls flirted. They did not know how to speak to a peasant.

He remained apart, answering direct questions as briefly as possible and otherwise remaining silent.

Jane succumbed on the next visit, and took the runner into the House and then to her room. When they rejoined the group, the runner stood apart, and Jane walked out into the gardens. The others stared and wondered, and their excitement was intense. Margaret was rather peeved that Jane should have taken what belonged to her, so she thought, because she had been the first to go to see him. She was determined not to wait any longer, and took the runner to her room.

During the night, he was taken to every room in turn, to some rooms more than once, and to some with more than one companion.

At dawn, the runner left the house and walked back to the village. The peasants watched secretly from their windows. Some of them made the priest's sign as he went past.

Some whispered that it was shameful to allow oneself to be so used, so abused. And they did not even get the presents that he used to give to their daughters, for he now spent all his time at the House. Others were not sure who was using whom.

In the autumn, as they sprawled around the fire one evening, he announced that he would run again.

All was prepared.

At three o'clock, the naked figure that they knew so well appeared on the lawn, saluted the group. The girls applauded vigorously. The peasants stared in silence. The secretary dropped his hand and the group moved for the guns. The runner waited and then dashed for shelter.

Time after time he raced and darted from one side of the clearing to the other. Time after time they shot and missed as he swerved and crouched.

The light was fading as he came out for the twentieth dash. As he ran he hesitated. At that instant Charles fired.

"My God," said Charles, "I winged him."

The girls drew breath sharply.

"I've hit him," shouted Charles, as he saw the runner slow and stagger. "I've hit him."

The runner pressed his wound. He looked up at the terrace, saw the tense stares of the Friends. He heard their rapid breathing. He heard the silence from the woods.

The girls pressed around Charles excitedly. He felt them push against him, smelt their excitement, felt their hands reach for him.

"He's mine," he called and fired.

The runner twisted, clutched at his shattered body and fell to the ground.

Charles turned greedily to the girls, surveyed their burning faces.

"Next," called Thomas sulkily.

※ ※ ※

Amputation

A tale of survival

They say that a person who has lost an arm or a leg, even just a finger or a toe, may feel it still, may try to scratch the gap where their flesh should be. They say that they may sob in the night with the pain of something no longer there.

How much more so a mother who has lost her child? She will wake when she hears it whimper, or when she feels it tug at her useless breasts. And her first thought in the morning, every morning, is for that scrap of flesh which is never there. Such pain is as permanent as the loss itself.

* * *

Even if you first caught sight of Rachel in the crowded centre of the busy industrial town in which she lived, you would guess immediately that she was foreign. In contrast to the rather sloppy, noisy, hearty women around her, she was neat, small, brittle, like a bird in a cage, a cage that perhaps protected rather than confined her. She dressed differently, she looked different, and when she spoke, there was no doubt that she came from far away: no friendly, lilting accent but a flat, staccato stream of odd consonants and guttural vowels.

She moved among others like a spot of oil on water, perhaps wishing to mix, but held apart. She was marked out by a pain so overwhelming, so constant, that little else seemed to register in her mind. She walked, shopped, talked like a sleepwalker. Something knew what she was doing, but it wasn't really her.

Her loss was always there, always in the forefront of her mind. She coped as best she could. What else was there to do? But the worst trial would come each day as she walked to and from work. Each weekday morning, she would walk up the quiet terraced street, the noise of her heels echoing between the closed, unsmiling walls, with now and again the shout and the bell and the rattle of the milkman pushing his trolley up the middle of the street, or the laboured whine of a bus on its way to the centre. Women might already be scrubbing doorsteps, polishing the brass, cleaning windows. She moved in silence, dreading what was to come.

At the end of the street, she turned left, then right, and then sometimes, on bad days, she had to stop to try and control her emotions.

The road crossed a deep cutting in which the railway line ran. The trains brought coal from the mines to the docks or took copper, timber, a thousand things to the factories that sprawled all over the area. A steam engine was busy shunting wagons. There was the hiss of escaping steam, the great gasps as the wheels span on the tracks, the rhythmic clickety-click of a thousand wheels running over the joints in the rails, and, worst of all, the sound that would make her stop, doubled up in pain, that unique sound as the engine connected with a line of waiting wagons, and the steel buffers crashed together with a sound like that of empty bottles striking each other. The first wagon contacted the second, and the second struck the third, and the third the fourth and so on and so on, perhaps a hundred times. It was like a waterfall of tempered steel, countless slivers of high-pitched sound cutting into her brain, blades slicing into her raw, bleeding flesh.

At the end of the day, the torment was repeated. Out of the docks, along the crumbling quays of the river where dredgers lay, half rotten and rusting, past the chapel and the terraced houses, one of which had a tiny shop in its front room, and up the hill to the bridge over the railway. Already she could hear the steam engine, the cascading clash of buffers, like glass smashed on a kitchen floor.

She would lean against the railings through which you could look down on the tracks, and where sometimes an earnest boy sat collecting engine numbers.

She would arrive home distraught, hearing the cry of her child in every room. Dai would be waiting, unable to console her. What could he offer? An arm around her shoulder, unquestioning love, a few words.

"Dere 'ma, cariad. Come on, girl."

* * *

In earlier days, so many years ago, so many miles away, the railway line had crossed the end of the street on which she lived, where the shops and houses and workshops ended, and the warehouses and sidings began. The express trains would rush past, would blow their whistle, as if they knew she was waiting. Two short toots and a long wail that trailed off as they hurried away to Berlin, Leipzig, Prague, Warsaw, Vienna or Budapest, carrying exotic, glamorous passengers on a thousand adventures.

Her town swarmed with life: early morning traders headed to market; stolid horses pulled carts, watched over by a man in black, hat on head, long white whiskers falling onto his chest; boys with side-curls and high buttoned tunics; serious young men in long coats striding out to save the world; old men with beards, deep in discussion; groups chatting; old ladies with white caps; young women in print dresses, rich black hair in buns; unshaven workers; dour matrons. A thousand people laughing, arguing, talking. The old were from a world that had already gone; the young were hoping for a better world to come. And everywhere there were children, like rain running down a window after a sudden summer shower.

When the express raced past in winter, she would already be with her family, safe around the fire in their room. As the plaintive whistle trailed off into the cold night, her parents would check the clock, and send her to bed. In summer, the express would pass when they were all out in the street. Somewhere the sound of a violin or an accordion would strike up, and soon some would dance. The men would talk and argue; the women would knit or sew, sitting on chairs dragged out from their houses; the children would play. When the express whistled, the children were sent to wash and pray and leap into bed, to have the express carry them away in their dreams.

Rachel, a musical child, often spent her nights at the opera in Vienna. Dressed in a stunning, full-length silk gown, with diamonds around her neck, coils of black hair framing her pale face, she would be greeted by a huge man, handsome, charming, slightly roguish with a black beard and a flashing gold tooth. He bowed to her, and she nodded gracefully. And later they would dance, and young men would look longingly at her, timidly address a few words to her, and would blush as she graced them with the slightest smile, until another train would whistle, and whisk her back to her own bed.

* * *

Years and childish dreams passed. She did not get to the opera in Vienna. But as she grew, young men did look longingly, did blush, did address their words to her. Eventually she chose not a huge man with a black beard, but a slight, young school-teacher who argued about art and politics and history, and who passionately clutched her to him at night.

Time passed. Her body swelled, and her smile took on that sublimely distant look that comes to some with pregnancy. A boy was born, and the family celebrated, and she was lulled by the infant sucking on her breast.

The trains still whistled as they passed, but no longer did she dream of the opera. They would lie awake at night, hearing a dog howling, the ring of boots on cobbles, the chanting of a mob. Sometimes there would be a scream, maybe even a shot.

When the silence of the night settled again, she would rise furtively and go to the cot. How could such a scrap incite so much hatred? It was ludicrous that grown men should dress up and rant and rave about her and her child. But there was nothing funny in stars daubed on shop-fronts, in old men beaten in the streets, in women who no longer dared go out, in hate-filled rallies and marching boots.

Yet the baby's laughter fell like a blessing.

One winter night, the sound of the marching boots stopped just when it was at its loudest. For a moment, all was silent. Then the door of their house burst open in a volley of shouts and curses. Men poured into the bedroom with a clatter of boots and rifles and oaths, and her husband was dragged from the bed, hurled to the floor, kicked, beaten, dragged away. Jewish whore, they shouted, hating, leering, lusting, and they pulled the filthy whore from her bed, handled her, beat her, pushed her into the street. The baby's cries rose like an accusation to the heavens.

All along the street, doors were kicked in, windows smashed. Furniture, books, clothes, even people, were hurled from windows onto the icy cobbles. Flames rose from one house where an oil-lamp had shattered on the floor. Serious men, only ever seen in black suits and tall hats, shivered with spindly legs in strange nightshirts; children cried and huddled against each other; outraged matrons protected their modesty as best they could; young men wished that for just one minute they had the guns that were pointed at them.

One old man clung to the doorpost of his house as the soldiers kicked and beat him, smashing his hands with the butts of their rifles. Still, he held on. He would not go. An officer stepped forward, shouted an order. The soldiers stood back, and the officer drew his pistol. He put it to the old man's forehead, right between his eyes. Yet still he clung desperately to the post. The officer pulled the trigger.

"So, stay!" the officer sneered.

He bent down to wipe the barrel of his pistol, soiled with blood and brains, on the old man's coat.

Men in greatcoats prodded the people with their rifles, cursed, kicked, laughed and drove them off down the lane towards the railway tracks, like ill-trained sheep.

Those whose turn had not yet come peeped at this grim midnight procession. A mother's scream rose above the other noises as, from her window, she saw her son in the street. Arms grabbed her to stop her rushing out.

As they got to the end of the lane, opposite the warehouses and the wagons waiting on the tracks, one man ran for his life. Orders rang out, shots were fired, and some soldiers pursued the young man.

Amid this confusion, a shutter creaked open, and a voice whispered urgently.

"Quick, give me the baby."

She turned slowly, not understanding.

"Quick," the voice urged. "They'll kill him."

She clutched the child closer to her.

The soldiers came back, dragging a body along the ground behind them.

"The only chance."

Desperate, desolate, she passed the baby in through the scarcely opened shutter. The shutter creaked closed, and she heard the bars drop into place. She stood, arms hanging uselessly, empty. Somebody put an arm around her shoulder, forced her to turn away, to shuffle on with the crowd being forced to the waiting wagons.

Families were split up. Lovers were torn from each other. Couples whispered their final farewells. Prayers were muttered. Children cried.

But not hers. At least not for her ears.

* * *

It was nearly four years before she returned to that place. Not much was left. Piles of broken bricks, jagged pieces of wood, ruins already covered in weeds that put out gaudy flowers. Like neat sentinels, a row of doorsteps marked where their lives had once been led.

What had she been hoping for? A sleeping baby miraculously frozen in time? She didn't know. But there had to be something, not just this. No sign. No mark. No blood. No cry.

Doggedly, she went from office to office, from house to house, from village to village, from town to town, from grave to grave. Nobody knew what had happened to the neighbour or to her child. Nobody.

The child would perhaps have grown in silence and in darkness, among bits of half chewed food and whispered words, amid howls of despair in the night. Suffering would have become ingrained in his soul, like dirt on a schoolboy's knees.

The child would perhaps have been thrown onto a pile of anonymous, monstrous corpses where God himself had died.

She lay in the dirt, not thinking, not hoping, existing in a posthumous life. She was what glib politicians called a fortunate survivor.

As night fell, she felt a hand shake her gently, heard a voice call to her in some unknown tongue.

"Dere 'ma, cariad. Come on, girl."

* * *

Dai did not deal with abstract questions. It was not that he was ignorant. He knew the things he needed to know: how to grow crops in damp soil, how to fatten a pig, how to milk, how to make butter, how to make do with the little that nature conceded in his dark corner of the world.

He had been brought up in unsmiling poverty on a few acres. On a hillside far from the village, a house, some sheds, a pigsty huddled from the wind. The well was two fields away, down the hill. Cooking was done over a log fire which was never allowed to go out, day or night, summer or winter. This fire was the only source of heat for the family, and, if the winter was unusually hard, for the horse!

Dai knew about death. For months he watched as the pig grew and grunted happily with its snout in the damp earth. He cared for this carefree beast until the very minute when, with almost a lover's caress, he drew the blade across its throat.

Then the letter came, in a language he did not know, telling him to report to a place he did not know and for a reason he did not understand. It seemed that men, not pigs, were now to be led, impotently and innocently, towards death. It seemed that somebody had decided that Dai had to kill men, not pigs, and that Dai had to obey.

In the midst of a million deaths, it seemed even more important to save one life.

"Dere 'ma, cariad."

* * *

For days the train had lumbered on. The wagons were filled with the stink of other animals, which had also perhaps been conscious of the slaughter house at the end of the track.

People prayed, loved, died, despaired. Stripped of their former dignity, they acquired more dignity than ever. Old men tried to remember what things children liked, and, unable to do so, ruffled their hair, held them tight, told them it would be all right.

She noticed nothing as she rocked with grief, as she felt the mouth on her breast. She could feel the soft warmth, so soft, of that smooth skin, so warm. She could smell its milky breath, hear its gentle breathing, see the first smile, taste its flesh as she kissed it in endless love.

One morning, the train stopped. Soldiers emptied the wagons onto a cold flat land. Now and again they threw a corpse out onto the ground, or kicked and pushed an old woman until she fell to the ground where dogs snapped and snarled at her.

As she climbed down, she slipped. She felt a pair of hands grab her. But the hands did not let go. And she was passed from hand to hand, as they touched her, explored her, pulled open her coat to see her shivering body in her nightdress.

They were driven along a track towards a high wire fence. Gracefully curved concrete posts were strung with link fencing and barbed wire. Below the fence the gravel was weed free, raked like in a park in a city. They saw two towers flanking a wide gateway, more soldiers, dogs, and through the gateway, rows of huts as in some child's model village.

When the others were driven through the gate, she was taken to a hut beside the entrance. The door was thrown open and the soldier called out to the men inside, pushed her into the stifling hut. The soldiers advanced noisily, greedily towards her.

Some slavering animal used her, then another, and another and so on and so on. But while her body served for men's sport, her soul was absent. She waited only for the day when she would find her child.

And while millions died, she survived.

* * *

Dai had found her in a corner of a half-ruined hut.

"Dere 'ma, cariad," he said, and lifted her from the ground.

He took her to the camp, but they said she had already been processed, and closed their books and their hearts.

Dai did not understand the big questions, but a creature in pain needs help. What more is there to understand?

Dai found her a shelter, kept an eye on her, as does a

child who finds a bird with a broken-wing, who makes a nest for it in a shoe-box, who nurses it until the wing mends and it can be set free. But when it was all over for Dai, the wing had not mended, and so he took her back with him to a remote hillside.

After days on rattling trains, after the sea and the city, after a string of small towns dominated by smoke stacks, coal mines, flaming, belching factories, after drab streets of grimy houses climbing the hills, the train burst from a tunnel into the light, into a valley with a river curving through green fields. Then a ride in a car with no floor down rutted tracks and into a farmyard that stood outside of time.

Life was hard: the patterns of birth, life, decay and death were too obvious. The lottery of life was writ large on this forbidding land.

During the days, they worked. At night, they lay side by side. If desire came to him in the dark, its fulfilment was rapid and summary, like that of casual strangers. So desire soon declined, and they slept side by side, huddled in their own dreams and nightmares.

Dai had few words, and his compassion was usually expressed in a silent smile. He knew that she would never fly again. And she knew she would never fly again. And she knew that this bleak shoe-box protected her, even if it did sometimes seem like a prison.

By day they fought the unresponsive soil, and eventually lost the fight. The green fields, the sheeting rain, the sparkling rainbows and dew-encrusted roses gave way to a cramped, mean life.

They moved to an industrial town like so many others,

to a street like so many others: long unbroken terraces with heavy front doors giving directly onto the street, with, now and again, a small shop in a front room, or a gloomy chapel, pompous and ugly. Beyond the houses were factories, docks, the tin-plate works, railway yards, warehouses, workshops. Far from his fields and woods, Dai sought refuge amongst pigeons and geraniums in a tiny back yard.

Dai worked in the tin-plate factory and was always teased for his country simplicity. She worked in a canteen at the docks, pouring cups of tea and slicing bread. Her life no longer cast a shadow.

On Saturdays, she would walk to the town centre to hear the noise and clamour of the trolley-buses and the hurrying crowds. She would move among the market stalls of fish and fruit, among smiling faces and endless chatter. She would get a cup of tea from the tall man with the beard who always said hello and asked how you were, as if he really remembered you among the thousands that passed along his counter each day.

On Sundays the town was quiet. No children laughed. No tales were told. Even the parks were locked up in case somewhere, in some small way, somebody might enjoy himself. Families went rigidly to chapel, best shoes clumping along the pavements under the sour scrutiny of old women on their Saturday scrubbed doorsteps. Mournful strains of sanctimonious men in three-piece suits singing gloomy hymns of damnation came from ugly chapels: ugly music from ugly buildings and from often ugly hearts.

Sometimes. when she walked home from work, there would be children playing in the streets, and she would go into the shop to avoid them. Prevarication at best, but it would delay crossing the railway, delay travelling back yet again to a street a thousand miles away.

She came out of the shop with a pound of apples. She plodded up the hill, staring ahead in fear and in defiance of that corner of the last house, of the few feet of railings that looked down onto the railway tracks. He was there again, that small boy, squatting on the ground, watching the engines, studiously copying down their numbers.

"Hello," he said, and smiled.

He would be about that age. Perhaps he was sitting somewhere, grubby knees in short trousers, writing down numbers.

The bag of apples slipped from her grasp, and they rolled away down the hill, rolling, bouncing down the gutter, out into the street, past the houses, down to the filthy, stinking, yellow river.

The boy set off in pursuit, gathering apples like Adam in a primitive Eden.

She watched for a moment, then sank to the ground. When the boy proudly came back with her apples, all except one which had eluded him, he found her crying with a desperate, heart-rending sound. He stared for a moment, then ran to the shop.

She lay there for a long time, the time it took the little boy to run to her house, to tell Dai, and to return. People stood in a semi-circle, impotently, watching her misery.

Gentle hands lifted her, and she heard that gentle voice.

"Dere 'ma, cariad."

❀ ❀ ❀

Game Over

A modern mystery

The mare's hooves thundered in time with his racing heart.

"Faster! Faster!" he urged, and pricked her on.

The sun glinted on the armour of the Black Knight racing towards him. Arthur squinted through his visor, lined up the lance, steadied himself on the mare's generous back, steeled himself for that shattering blow as the enemy tore at his breast. As they closed on each other, he kept the point up, rose and fell with the gallop, waited, waited, waited and thrust.

The pain exploded, and then was swamped by joy and relief as the Black Knight fell. Arthur pulled off his helmet to accept the acclamations, keenly searching for her face. Perhaps now he would be worthy.

Too late he heard the arrow sing, saw a black cape swirl as the marksman turned away. The arrow ripped through his throat, and everything went black.

"You have been killed."

The screen announced his fate impartially. Funereal music played, and then, with a fanfare of trumpets, the screen flashed in brilliant colours, asking that inevitable question.

"Would you like another life?"

Arthur glanced at his watch. It was almost midnight. He turned the machine off, and went into the bedroom where his wife was already asleep.

* * *

The next morning he glanced round his study guiltily, as if fearing that he would be found out. After all, the computer was supposed to be for work, and he was supposed to be working. He was already behind schedule.

"Would you like another life?" the screen asked.

He pushed the key.

The drive whirred and the red light flickered. Brilliant creatures leapt and danced for a moment, and then she appeared. Her skin was strangely pale, almost diaphanous. Her expression was subdued, haunted, beseeching. Then the screen cleared.

He didn't really know why he had bothered to buy the game. It was the unusual advertisement in the magazine that had caught his eye: goblins and dragons and wizards and warriors and indescribable beasts writhed on the page in a tangled, multi-coloured pyramid. This nightmare was woven around and over a woman of exquisite and haunting beauty: the hidden goddess.

"Find the goddess and discover the truth of life," the advert had proclaimed.

He had taken no further notice, but the next day he found himself wondering just how you discovered that elusive goddess.

So he daydreamed. So he picked up the phone.

At first he hadn't understood anything, and he could not see what he was supposed to do. There were so many different factors to take into account. The screen showed, with hallucinatory clarity and detail, an endless, scrolling map, with all sorts of people and objects and situations along its infinite paths. He soon discovered that many of the people, although they went about their own private business with maniacal intensity, were quite happy to ignore you, as long as you could contrive to stay out of their way. Others, however, seemed to have nothing better to do than to plot the downfall, by fair means or foul, of the frail and uncertain stranger wandering in their midst.

The computer silently recorded it all, kept account of your money, your experience, and, above all, of your life. Meters ticked away, and when they reached zero, you were dead. There was no appeal.

"You have been killed by the dragon," the machine announced.

The funereal music played, and then, with a fanfare of trumpets, the screen flashed in brilliant colours.

"Would you like another life?"

"You have been captured by the goblins and locked in their prison from which there is no escape."

The music played, the trumpets blared, the screen flashed.

"Would you like another life?"

Arthur died a hundred deaths. A hundred times, the dirge reverberated, the fanfare blasted, the screen flashed.

"Would you like another life?"

"Would you like a cup of tea, Arthur?"

He was startled by the voice calling up the stairs.

"Arthur?" his wife called again, "are you there?"

He turned the computer off and went down.

"Have you finished?" Jane asked.

"Yes," he answered, "almost, anyway. And you? Did you have a good day?"

* * *

The following day, he did a little better. He visited one village and bought a horse and some food. As he was negotiating for weapons with the blacksmith, he was attacked by a mob of peasants who accused him of the most heinous crimes. He leapt on his horse and was celebrating his getaway when he fell straight into the clutches of the forest spirits.

"You have been killed."

Dirge. Fanfare. Flashing colours.

"Would you like another life?"

Slowly he improved. He visited castles, drank of enchanted streams, confronted monsters, was beset by plagues. He battled with grasping politicians and vicious traitors, corrupt tyrants and desperately lascivious women. He collected swords and daggers, lances and shields, herbal salves and magic potions, money and talismen. He was wounded and healed, hated and loved, kissed in passion, and in innocent gratitude by those he had delivered from their torments. He solved problems, answered riddles, travelled through many lands, learned so much in this strange dialogue with the flickering specks on his screen.

He told his publisher that he was not well.

He told his wife that he had come up against a difficult problem and couldn't keep up.

"Good night," she would call out as she went to bed.

"Good night," he would reply, hastily resetting the computer in case she looked in.

* * *

From morning till night, he wandered through this magic world. Yet the object of the quest remained elusive. Nowhere could he find the face that peeped out wistfully at the start of every game. Once, in a small, dark room in a remote castle, he thought he had glimpsed a faint outline in the blackness of a wall. But it was only a fleeting image that he could neither fix nor recapture.

But that was his only clue, and so he found himself drawn back to the small room. By the time he could get there, his life meter was already low, and he was close to exhaustion and death. Every time he came back, he was wiser, older, but no closer to finding the goddess and the secret of life.

He inspected the walls, the floor, the ceiling, the doors, each piece of furniture. He knew them by heart. He had tried every way forward. He must have missed something.

His life meter ticked perilously low.

"I'm tired," he told the machine.

"Would you like to sleep for a while?"

"I don't understand what I am to do."

"Would you like to buy some advice from the magician?"

"No," he answered angrily. He had tried that before, had paid dearly for advice that had led him straight into a trap.

"I want the truth," he said.

"Truth? I'm afraid I don't understand," the machine answered.

"No, I bet you don't. You only know how to lie and cheat. The whole thing is fixed. You're a liar and a cheat," he shouted angrily.

The screen flickered for an instant. The face beckoned from the wall.

"There she is," he cried out. "That's her. I want her."

"I'm afraid I don't understand," the screen insisted.

The life meter flashed briefly.

"You have died of old age. You are becoming rather bad-tempered and quite anti-social," the screen announced in a gleeful postscript.

The funereal music droned out, the trumpets rasped, and the screen lit up brilliantly.

"Would you like another life?"

* * *

He was soon back in that black prison. A door on the left, a door on the right. A table, a chair, a rug. He had once spent an enormous amount of effort to move the furniture and roll back the rug. He had found a trapdoor that led to the cellars, an endless maze in which innocent children and tyrants, mothers and satyrs, the immaculate and the murderer, the sinner and those sinned against, rotted together in higgledy-piggledy agony.

He walked closer to the wall. He checked it inch by inch, but could find no clue, no reason why he had twice seen a faint image of her bewitching face in that inscrutable blackness.

"I want the truth."

"Truth? I'm afraid I don't understand."

"I want the goddess."

"I'm afraid I don't understand."

"I have seen her. I want her. She was here in this room."

"I'm afraid I don't understand."

"You're a liar. I want her."

"I'm afraid I don't understand."

"A liar. You're a miserable liar. I want the truth."

"Truth? I'm afraid I don't understand."

Arthur felt weary, defeated, drained. Enough was enough.

"I give up," he conceded, sitting back in his chair, his eyes heavy with tiredness. "I'm beaten. I give in."

"Are you certain?" the screen gloated.

It was midnight, and he would do better to go to bed. He waited for the music, the infuriating fanfare and the psychedelic flashing of the question.

The disc whirred, the red light flickered. The woman's face flitted across the screen, faded through the black wall. Then everything stopped. The life meter flashed and ticked to zero.

He stared in broken frustration. Then the wall moved. It came slowly closer, so close that the screen was filled with a blackness in which he could see the reflection of his own face, so close that it loomed over him, seemed to push its way right out of the screen, so close that the screen was like some deep, dark tunnel at the end of which he could just discern the faint lines of a face. He wavered, stumbled and fell forward into the blackness.

* * *

"You have come at last," she said, "I have been waiting for so long."

He glanced around nervously, fearing some trap, some treachery. They were standing in a sun-drenched garden. She was smiling, holding out her hand. He stepped forward gingerly. Their fingers touched, and he felt his being flow into hers. They turned and slowly walked away together.

By day they strolled hand in hand, and at night they lay together. Each day brought another form of paradise; each night a deeper form of bliss. In enchanted gardens, the perfumes of a million flowers elated them. The spray of crystal cascades drifted like the kiss of gossamer to cool them. Succulent fruits sustained and intoxicated them. Magic birds with brilliant plumage sang sweet songs. Around every corner was a new and different wonder with other inexhaustible joys.

They spoke little, for they did not need words. She knew his desires before he did, satisfied lusts he had not known he felt, led him where he would have wished to go, if he had had time to formulate that wish.

For what seemed like forever, they wandered through lands of entrancement. Each day contained the joy of a lifetime, and yet flew away in a second. Ecstatic nights gave way to dawn before they had had time to snuff the candle.

* * *

One day Arthur caught sight of a far-off castle on a hill.

"Who lives there?" he asked, startled by the sound of his own voice after so many days of unspoken communion.

"Nobody," she replied, and turned to lead him to a dappled glade where fish played in a sparkling stream.

He glanced at her in surprise.

"It is not a good place," she insisted, and urged him away.

Arthur hesitated, and turned back to look. He felt her hand let go of his to brush away a tear. A shadow flitted across her face as if a bird had crossed the sun. A leaf stirred in the wind. A thought stirred in his mind.

"I would just like to see it," he protested gently.

He walked on ahead. He kept turning round, but the sun was shining low under a gathering cloud, and it was sometimes difficult to see where she was, or even if she was there.

There was something strangely familiar about the castle. He strode with defiant resolution across the drawbridge, went through a low door, and found himself in a small, black room. A door on the left, a door on the right. A table, a chair, a rug. Arthur turned to face the blank wall. He walked closer, so close that he could touch it, so close that it closed over him.

* * *

He stared at the screen. All the meters were on zero. He waited for the funereal music, for the fanfare and for the question. But the screen remained still, with a message in drab monochrome at the bottom: GAME OVER

He bent forward and switched the computer off.

He must have slept.

He stood up, turned out the light, and quietly went downstairs. Jane was still up, he thought, as he caught sight of a gleam of light under the front room door.

He eased the door open and called her name. There was no answer, but the light wavered and he heard a cry.

He pushed the door, and stopped in surprise. Jane was sitting bolt upright, fully dressed, on a hard, kitchen chair, staring fixedly ahead. In front of her, a candle flickered, casting strange shadows in a grotesque dance around the room.

"Jane," he called out.

She did not answer.

"Jane," he whispered. "What's wrong? Why are you crying?"

She did not answer. She shivered, and pulled her shawl more closely about her. She turned as if to see what had caused a sudden, cold gust, and then she stared grimly ahead.

In the darkness, he could make out an open coffin, its rich wood glinting with deceptive warmth in the yellow, shuddering light. He walked up to the coffin hesitantly. He peered into the blackness and could see the shadowy mass of the body that lay futilely in the box. But it was not possible to see properly.

The candle guttered, and then burned more brightly. He leaned over, staring into the blackness of the deep, dark box in which he could now discern the faint outlines of a face -of his own face.

He stared in disbelief and in horror. He tried to step back, but he wavered, stumbled and tumbled forward. As the blackness closed over him, he caught sight for a moment of a weeping face shrouded in black, and then, as all went dark, he saw the drab message.

GAME OVER

✤ ✤ ✤

PERSON OR PERSONS UNKNOWN

*Obligations
on a noisy afternoon*

The solid, stolid city slept fast under its dark blanket. Curling arabesques of orange street lights hung in space. Occasionally headlights crept through the web, or a faint snatch of music was heard. Travellers who had turned uneasily in an unknown bed were now still. Lusts had been sated, or had abated. In the hospital, those who were to die that night had done so, and the others slept, not knowing, as yet, that they had survived to see another day. Even mothers slumbered.

As dawn came, the street lights paled against a lesser black, and a grey mist hung over the city like a shroud. Odd noises were heard: water dripped from trees, a starter motor complained; an engine coughed into life.

The sun appeared over the plains, bathing the tips of the steeples on the churches in a pink glow. The city inched its way back to life. A thousand eyes opened to the day. A few cried for those whose eyes would open no more.

Lorries carrying fresh produce to the markets lumbered through the streets; buses appeared, at first empty, but then packed with workers; dustcarts advanced fitfully, collecting droppings like mechanical dung-beetles. The smell of newly baked bread escaped from basement ovens. The laughter of children peeled out, punctuated by the syncopated tapping of high heels.

* * *

People clutched a life that they did not have time to question.

Horns blared in frustration as the roads became jammed. Housewives jostled and pushed in queues, and hurried home with their plastic bags, heaving themselves ungraciously up the steps of buses. Businessmen argued vigorously in cafes, strode self-importantly into banks where the doormen addressed them by name. Goods were bought and sold and sometimes stolen.

In the east of the city, the vast university campus was an oasis with lawns and trees around the stark modernist buildings. In one corner of the campus, a few streets of small houses with vegetable gardens and fruit trees sat incongruously in this context of another age and another scale.

Students hurried to their classes, to their friends, to the libraries, eager to collect those scraps of knowledge that might qualify them for a better job, even if not for a better life. Lecturers scurried shortsightedly, pranced pompously, sidled vaingloriously, and squinted sideways at the girls, or at their own reflected or imagined reputations.

But the campus lay besieged by a circle of roads that produced a constant roar of traffic, of sirens, of screaming brakes.

* * *

At midday, the rumble of traffic subsided briefly as the cars and trucks disappeared, like snow in the sun. The traffic lights were left to blink meaninglessly at empty roads like surreal insects. Orange buses glided silently along the deserted boulevards like modern ghost ships. The city slipped back into village ways. All was quiet. It was as if there was a chink in time.

Those who were reluctant to allow the summer to go sat outside to eat. From open windows, the tinkling of cutlery and the murmur of conversations rained onto the streets. A plump woman crossed the garden to recount the virtues of her latest lover to her neighbour, who tried to listen, but who could not stop her eyes flitting around lest a speck of dust might slip into her polished cage. From another window came the strident music that announced the television news, and a brittle voice rattled out with professional excitement the latest catalogue of murders and catastrophes, of people dying in new ways, and in ever increasing and ever more meaningless numbers.

In one of the old houses in the quiet, forgotten corner of the campus, an old lady dragged a chair out onto a balcony, whispered something to the canary that whistled energetically at her side, and settled to continue her crochet, and to remember the man who had been killed so long ago in a field somewhere. She stared vacantly at her neighbour who, clanking the gate shut, set off unhurriedly towards the university. Across the road, a tramp shifted, as timid and as sharp as a bird, from one dustbin to another outside the student refectory.

Drifting up from the valley, the distant wail of an ambulance interrupted this truce -perhaps the cry of birth, perhaps the scream of death.

Then, in the east, there was a deep rumble. The sound increased in volume until it was almost painful, making people cover their ears, making them unaware of everything apart from the noise. The ground shook.

Two black aircraft appeared, still low, still slow, and crossed over the campus. Two black deltas of death. As the planes changed direction, the rasping snort of the engines hurt like a blade.

When the planes had disappeared, it took a while to recover the sense of hearing. But any peace was lost, and time and noise reconquered their domain.

* * *

The back doors of the refectory burst open, and a group of women appeared, like a flock of brightly coloured birds. They chattered noisily, called out to each other as they went their different ways.

One hung behind, a long-legged, smiling figure. She looked around cautiously before walking over to the dustbins into which she dropped something. The tramp mumbled, and moved away, clutching the packet. Somebody called out her name, and she started, spun round, frightened that she had been caught.

A young man stepped forward.

"You frightened me," she complained. "What are you doing here?"

"I said I would come," he protested meekly.

They embraced, the intended warmth of the man's embrace rebuffed by her brusque peck.

"I thought you had classes."

"I do," he said, and he glanced at his watch.

"Won't you get into trouble?"

"Nobody cares."

In his right hand, he held an open, bulging, battered briefcase that showed books and papers untidily pushed inside. He slipped his arm around her waist.

"You're not going to start all that again, are you?" she demanded. "Everybody's watching."

She turned her head to gesture at the windows of the refectory where, in fact, a couple of people were standing and staring idly down. He did not turn to look, but gazed sullenly at her.

"Well?" she continued with false gaiety, "what are you doing here?"

He stared at her in silence.

"Cat got your tongue? Come on then, you can walk with me to the bus-stop. But you'd better hurry. I'm going dancing."

And she set off across the campus.

"Why don't you come?"

"I can't," he replied.

"Why not?"

"I can't." He hesitated. "I thought you were coming with me this afternoon."

She tensed, but made no answer. She quickened her step and strode on determinedly.

"It's a lovely day," she said.

She threw back her shoulders, breathed deeply of the cool, dry air, turned her face to the sun and let its warmth caress her freckled face. Then she strode on jauntily, refusing to let his tempo dominate.

A distant rumble could be heard from the east.

His mind and body were like a dead weight.

"I've got to see you," he blurted out.

"Well, here I am," she smiled innocently, defiantly.

The rumble was approaching, growing, filling the sky like thunder, or some angry god.

"You can't keep putting me off like this."

The noise swelled suddenly. Two aircraft thundered over the buildings, climbed and then turned away. As they turned the pitch of the noise was lowered as the full force of the blast was hurled against the city.

He ranted on as if in some poorly done dumbshow. She turned to him, spread her hands, pointed up at the sky, mouthing that it was impossible to hear.

"You've got to," he screamed at the top of his voice, leaning towards her, hating the planes that mocked him thus.

"You've got to."

* * *

"You've got to. ..."

James broke off in mid-sentence as the planes roared over. He mouthed a curse, joined his hands on his lecture notes, rolled his eyes heavenwards, and waited with a look of pained patience on his face. Playing to the gallery as usual.

He glanced down at his watch, and stifled a yawn.

The gallery did not seem too impressed. Some fifty or sixty students -not a bad turnout for a sunny day, he thought- were spread around the room according to the intricate rituals of student lore. The merely bored sat at the back; those who wanted to learn, but not to be seen to want to do so, sat in the middle; those who were desperate to learn sat in the front, together with those who were aggressive about their total lack of interest, and for whom it was compulsory to make a show of reading or playing cards or talking throughout the lecture. One of them had even come in on his bicycle once!

He walked over to the windows that were shaking with the effect of the aircraft. It was still bright and sunny. The trees and bushes dotted around on the lawns below him flaunted their colours. Some sixty yards away the glass walls of the library glinted like some monolithic jewel inside which you could see people going about their tasks. On the path below, a handful of students were strolling lazily away from the campus towards the main road on which the traffic was once again busy.

"Obligations. As I was saying," he continued, having returned to his desk, "today we shall deal with obligations, of which there are three types."

He waited to let it all sink in, or at least be written down.

"They are, as you no doubt know, positive obligation, negative obligation and absence of obligation. And the verbs which express obligation in English are ...", and he paused and looked around the group for an answer that he knew would not be forthcoming. But it changed the rhythm, broke the tension, released the concentration for a moment. He studied the faces that stared back at him in silence.

"The verbs which express obligation are 'must', 'have to' and 'need'. So before we consider the various uses of these verbs, let us remind ourselves of their forms."

Again, he paused and looked round the room.

"And although the English spend their lives hedged around by endless obligations, the main verb in their language to express obligations, 'must', is incomplete."

He glanced up, but nobody had understood, perhaps nobody had even noticed his would-be witty comment.

"So," he continued, rather disappointed, "the form 'must' is used to express obligation for all persons in the present and future tenses. The negative is 'must not' and the interrogative is 'must I?' It has no other forms. It is followed by the infinitive without 'to'."

"So far so good. However," and he breathed deeply,

"as there are no other forms of 'must', all other tenses must be supplied by the verb 'to have to'. This verb may also be used in the present and future tenses, but its meaning in these tenses is not the same as the meaning of 'must'."

"The negative and the interrogative of 'to have to' may be formed either according to the rules for auxiliary verbs, or according to the rules for ordinary verbs, that is, either with or without the auxiliary 'do'. Whenever the auxiliary 'do' is not used, the word 'got' may be added and in this case 'have' usually contracts."

"Thus, the negative is either 'You haven't to', or 'You don't have to' or 'You haven't got to'."

"The interrogative is either 'Have you to?' or 'Do you have to?', or 'Have you got to?'."

"The positive is 'You have to', or 'You do have to,' or 'You've got to."

"Any questions?" he asked defiantly.

It was the seventh time already that he was retailing his lecture, and he had another three to go. Ten groups of a hundred students each, nominally at least, who were supposedly mastering the intricacies of the English language. Sometimes he would find it difficult to hold on to reality as he repeated the same words -and, for all he knew, to the same faces.

When he felt himself sinking, he would ask for questions, and walk to the window to recover his senses.

People were hurrying along the paths below the window. A large group waited at the bus stop by the traffic lights where a stream of traffic raced by. Even through the windows, he could hear the constant grumbling of wheels and brakes and engines.

The sun still shone brightly, but the colour was fading and the light was thinner and colder. The old lady in the house next door would be taking her canary in soon, he thought.

He released the catches, and pushed the large window. The noise surged in, assaulting the island of peace. The cold, fresh air raced in like life itself, and he gasped greedily at it. For a few moments, he stared at the passers-by, watched two African boys laughingly accost a group of girls. Back to obligations, he sighed. He walked back to the desk.

"In the present and future tenses, both 'must' and 'to have' may express positive obligations. However, 'must' usually implies that the speaker approves of, or has created the obligation, whereas 'to have' relates the obligations created by an external authority. Consider, for example, the differences in 'You must obey the law,' and 'You have to obey the law.'

* * *

She was about twenty-three or four. Her features were rather plain, rather flat, but she was provocative. She was a little overweight, and that gave a roundness, a ripeness to her body that was exciting. She was completely at ease in her skin, totally aware of her body, and yet unselfconscious about it. Her pleasures and her boredom were physical rather than intellectual.

He was younger: twenty perhaps, perhaps even less.

Although he was not physically unattractive, there was something about his timidity that grated.

Yet one morning he had woken in her bed, confused and incredulous, drained both physically and mentally. She had made coffee, and sat wrapped in a dressing gown, chattering brightly about this and that.

She seemed to show no traces, gave no clues, as she poked at a sugar lump to make it dissolve more quickly. The reality of her nakedness as she started to dress shocked him, and this sagging, dumpy flesh was more intimidating in the sober light of morning than when caressed in his fantasies.

What was inconsequential for her was essential for him. The frantic, furious intensity of his lust did not match her indolent pleasures. His violence, his desperate longing provoked her sighs of contentment, her grunts of desire. So he clung tenaciously, while she sipped her coffee and went carefree to her work and to other pleasures.

"You've got to," he shouted.

She shrugged, mouthed the fact that she could not hear, and set off again. He hurried after her, trying to make her stop by pulling at her arm.

"Listen," he called. "Listen. Please."

She jerked her arm free, and carried on walking.

"You've got to."

She stopped suddenly, turned to face him.

"You must."

"Don't keep telling me what I do and don't have to do," she snapped. "I don't owe you anything and you don't owe me anything."

He stared in disbelief.

"I am going to miss my bus. And what's wrong with you anyway? Hanging around like this. Haven't you got any friends?"

"But you are my friend," he answered.

"All right. But I'm going to miss my bus."

She started to hurry down the path across the car park and behind the lecture halls. He raced after her.

"But you can't. Not now," he said.

"What?"

He did not answer. He could not bring himself to say the words.

She turned away and walked on. Twenty yards away the traffic roared past, a stream of cars and lorries and motorbikes. Pedestrians also hurried by, caught up by the frenetic activity on the roads. She saw her bus go past. She sat down on a bench. She might as well get it sorted out now.

At a window in the lecture block, a face stared down. Then the face turned and disappeared.

* * *

"Now if you thought that the forms of 'to have to' were bad, just wait for the forms of 'to need'."

Nobody stirred.

"Firstly, 'to need' may mean 'to require', as in the sentence 'He needs a new car'. In such cases, it is a regular verb: 'need, needed, needed'. But 'to need' may also express a lack of obligation, as in 'He need not go'. In this case it is an auxiliary verb and often forms its negative and interrogative without 'do', for example 'Need I learn all this?'."

"However, 'to need' may also form its negative and interrogative forms with the auxiliary 'do'.

"So, the following are all correct forms to express an absence of obligation:

'He needn't do it. He doesn't need to do it. He doesn't have to do it. He hasn't got to do it.'

Any questions?"

He turned the catches, and pushed at the massive pane. It swung open a few inches. The air was becoming cold now. It bore a smell of exhaust fumes and wood fires that was welcome after the smell of so many tired bodies.

The noise was barely tolerable. It was impossible to think, to concentrate, to keep your mind free of this intrusion.

* * *

"You must," he shouted, his head spinning. "You've got to."

She didn't answer, no longer knowing how to respond to his insistence. She got up to leave.

"What I do or don't do has nothing to do with you. Just leave me alone."

He didn't move. He stared up at her. She looked at him and turned to go. For a few seconds, he sat as if paralysed.

"Just a minute. Wait."

He stumbled along the path after her.

"Please," he implored.

She stopped, turned, looked at him, and then carried on her way.

He was hunting desperately for something in his briefcase, dropping books and papers in his clumsy haste. He called out again, but his words could not be heard. He reached out to grab her shoulder, but she was too far in front. He reached down into his case, found the pistol, closed his eyes with the pain of the noise, and fired.

She stumbled, lurched to the left, and fell into a bush. He looked around in surprise, unable at first to understand where she had gone.

The noise of the planes slowly diminished, to be replaced by the noise of the traffic.

Then he understood. He looked around, but nobody was paying any attention. The buildings stared down impassively with their blind eyes. The traffic roared on. He had no idea what to do, so he turned the gun and fired again.

The noise of the second shot pierced even the students' awareness. Many of them rushed to the windows. James followed. The windows of the library opposite were also lined with curious faces. There was nothing to be seen.

He noticed that the lovers had gone, and that somebody had dropped papers and books on the grass.

The students returned to their seats reluctantly, and he resumed the lecture.

* * *

The wail of a siren rose up through the din with its harsh falsetto. Then it died abruptly. The students rushed to the window again. A van was parked on the grass and policemen were hurrying about. A crowd began to gather. Another siren wailed.

He turned from the window. Another five minutes yet.

"Negative obligation is expressed by 'must', and by certain forms of 'to have to '. Whereas 'you needn't' or 'you don't have to' express a lack of obligation, the negative of 'must' expresses an obligation not to do something. 'You must not do that'."

"Finally, 'must' followed by a perfect infinitive expresses a present deduction about a past action, 'He must have done it'.

By contrast, if the negative of 'need' is followed by a perfect infinitive it means that an action was unnecessary, but was nevertheless performed, 'he needn't have done it'."

He glanced at his watch.

"But we will come to that next time. Thank you for your attention."

* * *

When he left the building there was nothing to be seen on the grass below the window. The noise was still intolerable, and he walked quickly along the street towards his house. With each step, the noise faded, and when he reached his gate, he heard the whistling of the canary on the balcony next door. He looked up and saw the old lady huddled asleep over her crochet. He pushed the gate open and went in.

* * *

The squeal of the gate woke her up with a start. She stared around in surprise and then shivered.

"Come on," she said to the canary. "We'll catch our death."

She went into the room and pulled the shutters tightly closed.

❋ ❋ ❋

The Tussie-Mussie

A world of pastel passion

It was to be appreciated that even these days, despite the crassness and the strident commercialism of modern society, people of refined manners and good taste still existed. For that, at least, she was grateful, although if he were not a gentleman, things would not have got as far as they had, and she would not be in her current quandary.

He had passed by earlier that morning, silently, carefully laid the bouquet and card on the table, smiled and left. The bouquet was of roses, while the card showed a delightfully old-fashioned painting of a rose surrounded by tulips of various hues, a carnation in bud, all intertwined with violets.

Could a declaration be any clearer? The question could not be more apparent. The reply was to be found in the bouquet of roses: yellow, orange, pink and white blooms, and one glorious red rose in the centre. It was a bloom both demure and unspoiled, and not quite ....

She flushed a little, looked around in embarrassment as she sought the word. Full? Mature? Ready? Ripe? Indecorous images tried to slip into her most decorous mind, but she drove them out.

The declaration was clear. Her reply was not. Everything depended on which rose she put at the centre of the tussie-mussie. She knew that. He knew that. However, that did not solve the problem.

* * *

They had been lucky this year. "The Ladies' Tussie-Mussie and Floral Watercolour Society" had been given the first stand on the left after the entrance. Of course they would not draw crowds, as would the hamburger stalls, or the jewellery made from sunflower seeds, or those twee house names on slate. They would have fewer, but more discerning visitors.

For once, the weather was fine, and the setting, in the large meadow, bordered on three sides by the gently flowing river, and ringed by wooded hills and the old stone town nestled on the slope in front of the jagged ruined walls of the castle, was indeed idyllic. On such a wonderful day, the rows of stalls covered in striped green and white awnings looked positively jolly, although she was not totally in agreement about the clusters of bright blue balloons fastened above each display which, so the committee had decreed, would create a festive air.

She placed the roses in a tall vase at the centre of the table. The display itself was a work of art: elegant watercolours, all in matching frames and on small easels, vases of flowers, sketchbooks artfully arrayed, a scattering of decorative objects: pebbles, blades of grass, ears of corn, tubes of paint, slim long-handled brushes. In the centre, on an easel a little larger than the others, the painting of last year's tussie-mussie, created, as every year, on the day and at the fair, and one of her better ones, even if she said so herself. For a moment, her fingers lingered on the red rose, brushing the soft petals, testing the thorns, and she breathed deeply of its rich perfume.

"Rose", she sighed as she remembered the poem. *"Rose, who dares to name thee?"*

Each year, she thought, nature would shake off the cold bonds of winter, and spring would triumph again in a myriad of ways, the most wonderful of which was in flowers. Here was nature's greatest beauty, its sweetest smile, its most sublime joy, a delight for all the senses. Their perfume is incense sent to Heaven; their touch, balm for aspirant souls; their look, a mystery never to be fathomed; their tastes enriching a thousand dishes.

And for those who know how to hear, they speak of tenderness, of sorrow, of passion, at times profound, at times light-hearted. But they speak in subtleties and whispers unheard by common ears. They commune in delicate, perfumed silence, when spoken words would grieve a stricken soul.

She gazed at the bouquet, listened to its gentle urgings: the red rose sighing with passionate longing; the wanton orange with its urgent, sensual dream of fulfilment; the yellow offering friendship unsullied by desire; the white, the virgin white, whispering of a higher love, an innocent love guarded by silent virtue and purity.

What human voice could speak so gently, what words so beautifully?

"A rose is a rose is a rose, and by any other name," she sighed.

*"If on creation's morn the king of heaven
To shrubs and flowers a sovereign had given,
beauteous rose, he had anointed thee
Of shrubs and flowers the sovereign to be ...."*

"Excuse me."

*"The spotless emblem of unsullied truth,
The smile of beauty and the glow of youth
The garden's pride, the grace of vernal bowers, ..."*

"Excuse me," the intruding voice insisted.

"The blush of meadows ...."

A finger pointed up at the sign over her head.

"Excuse me. What is a tussie-mussie?"

Jane was called back from her delicious reverie by an elderly couple, pretentious in city-smart country clothes, gawping with the vacant, condescending smile of tourists.

"I say, you were far away. I wondered if you could tell us what this tussie-mussie thing is."

Jane smiled at her visitors, a professional smile that formed on her lips if not in her eyes.

"A tussie-mussie," she explained, "a tussie-mussie is a special kind of nosegay."

"Ah, I see," he said, although he didn't. "A nose-what?"

"A nosegay. A posy."

Faced with the blank looks, she persisted dutifully.

"A posy is a small circular arrangement of flowers made to be carried in the hand. Like bridesmaids have at a wedding."

She pointed out various graceful paintings, all of them by members of the society, and very reasonably priced.

"So what's the difference between a posegay and a tussie-thingy?"

"No. A posy or a nosegay. They look similar, but a posy is purely decorative, whereas a nosegay is designed for its perfume. Now a tussie-mussie ..."

"I say, look, Hester," the man interrupted, "there's a fellow making love spoons over there."

And they hurried off in search of the genuine original locally hand-crafted organic ethnic traditional love spoon.

* * *

Jane stood at the back of the stall, underneath the discreet sign with the society's name and its motto:

> *"By all those token flowers, that tell*
> *What words can never speak so well."*

She was an imposing figure, impressive if not inviting. She had grown from a sturdy, graceless child into a tall woman, solid, unyielding. She had a high waist, so that there was less distance from shoulder to waist than from waist to crotch, a peculiarity emphasised by her dark brown loosely fitting trousers that had a hint of jodhpurs about them. The trousers ended rather comically about four or five inches above her ankles, and she wore white socks and sensible flat pumps. A beige round-neck pullover, with the scalloped collar of a white blouse, decorated with flower motifs, showing around the neck, completed her outfit. Her hair was quite short, parted, bobbed. She wore no cosmetics.

She was strangely, disconcertingly sexless, like those Michaelangelo statues that are not quite right, with unconvincing lumps instead of breasts, and a worrying lack of genitalia. As a young woman, she had always been embarrassed by her menstruation, and she was glad when her periods had stopped, which they had done at an early age.

She had been up since five. Saturday was always the busiest day at the hotel, with the routine of breakfast, laundry, cleaning, with guests leaving and arriving. Everything had to be just right, and, in her experience, there was only one way of guaranteeing that things would be just right. So she did more than she should have herself.

On top of that, this was the day of the Art and Craft Fair. As President and Founder Member of "The Ladies' Tussie-Mussie and Floral Watercolour Society" she was in charge, choosing what to display, how to display it, loading. unloading, setting up, and making sure that everything was just right.

Her standards, as everybody always said, were very high.

That was how she had been brought up. Never accept anything less than perfection. She applied this rule to everything, to the hotel, to her painting, to the tussie-mussies, even to the few suitors who had now and again, though briefly, troubled her serenity.

On top of that, he was there: not intrusive, for he never was, but expectant. She had not had time to speak to him at the hotel, beyond the usual politenesses, but later he had called at the stand, put the bouquet and the card on the table, and left without a word.

Neither intrusive nor assertive, but he wanted an answer.

She had to get on. Every year she set herself the task of making a tussie-mussie, and then of producing a painting of the arrangement.

Although when she looked round at the visitors, she sometimes wondered why she bothered. Many did not appear to understand any language at all, without her trying to introduce them to the subtle language of flowers. Fat-thighed, adolescent girls; surly youths skulking under grimy hoods; effete accents braying noisily; bemused husbands trailing behind their clucking wives; bored tourists wondering why they hadn't gone to Spain and hoping never to see another steam railway.

Yet that was no reason to compromise. Her stall would be perfect, arranged with symmetry, precision, good taste. Virtue is its own reward, she always said.

She worked patiently and painstakingly on the flowers. Now and again, she was interrupted by a polite question, or by a kind comment on the year's efforts of a handful of fragile ladies. Jane explained how a subtle variation in flowers, in colours, in combinations, in position, in composition could make the difference between a declaration of a consuming, feverish passion and a polite rebuke that, while acknowledging the interest shown, discouraged any further enquiry. What different worlds were conjured up by these dainty ladies in a thorn here or there, in the angle of a stem, in a sprig of rue or thyme.

And, of course, the inevitable question! Did nobody know the word nowadays?

"A tussie-mussie," she explained repeatedly, "is like a posy, but with a rose at its centre that conveys a message."

As she sat and worked, she struggled with her quandary: with what colour rose should she respond to his declaration?

They had known each other for over 20 years. He had been one of the first guests at the hotel, and he had returned every year since. He was a fastidious gentleman, precise, polite, predictable, a neat solicitor from a small Midlands town, unmarried, untempted, reticent. For two weeks each summer, he traded his pin-stripe suits for tweeds and waders, and strolled around the countryside, poked his nose into antique shops, went fishing. He was one of those beings who leave little trace when they finally depart this world: a tidy will, hopeful relatives, a client annoyed because he needed him to remember the details of some ancient transaction, a sock and underwear drawer with all the items neatly arranged in rows, stamp albums with sets from Commonwealth countries all impeccably organised.

Not that she had been brought up to run a hotel. The imposing building, built as the family residence in earlier, more affluent times, stood on a hill, overlooked the town that clustered around the ruins of the castle. This castle had for so long been the seat of her family's power, while the rich meadows and fertile fields had been the source of their wealth for almost a thousand years.

She had had, and would no doubt be the last to have a charmed childhood in that house. She had been the only child, safe in a private world of lawns, water-gardens, groves, paddocks, peacocks, protected by half-timbered gate houses that straddled the three roads leading into the property. This special world had been peopled by kindly gardeners, cooks, servants, stable-boys, farm labourers who all proclaimed that she was the paragon of all virtues.

However, generations of youthful follies in foreign cities, and of expensive indiscretions had sapped the family fortunes. Her ancestors had no doubt been excellent anglers, humorous raconteurs, tempestuous lovers, now and again even scholars. Yet for too long, none of those talents had been turned into hard cash. Suddenly times were hard, labour was expensive, rents were low, and subversive political ideas destroyed the unquestioning respect and obedience to which the family had been accustomed ever since some Norman had murdered, burned and looted his way to wealth and prominence. To keep up their position, a farm was sold here, some cottages there. Servants were released, the gardens left to run wild. And then there was nothing left to sell, there were no more economies to be made.

Jane's father was superbly disinterested in this precarious situation. After all, there was no son to carry on the proud name. "Après moi le déluge", he was often heard to mutter. Her mother didn't think about the situation at all, for she had not been brought up to think, and had never acquired the habit.

Jane had to be rather more interested. She was over forty, with few prospects, with no means of support, and with two irresponsible parents fiddling while Rome burned. Unworldly as she was, she took control, decreed that the house should be turned into a hotel, that they would move into the gardener's cottage.

Nobody liked the thought that the descendants of mighty war-lords would be reduced to smiling politely and to cooking kippers for dentists and shop-keepers, that the famous water-gardens, around which political and ecclesiastical appointments had been decided for centuries, would be invaded by urchins who would throw stones and chase the ducks, that phoney country squires with split-cane rods and four-wheel drive vehicles should trample over their estate.

But what alternative was there? They were broke. Was she to be a shop-assistant? A genteel companion for incontinent old ladies? What would happen when she herself became an incontinent old lady? Whereas with a hotel, she insisted, they could run a select, discreet, refined establishment for select, discreet and refined guests.

So she sat at an elegant desk, alert, watchful, polite, yet aloof. On their first morning, guests would appear for breakfast, would greet her, and she would reply with a brief nod, a rapid good morning, almost, but not quite, a smile.

She feared the havoc that the guests would create in

the breakfast room. Her liking for order and decorative niceties became a compulsion. The tables were laid with fine linen tablecloths, gleaming silverware at precise right angles to the edge of the table and in the strictest order, sparkling glasses in the correct positions, fine china, serviettes folded sometimes in classical patterns, and sometimes, when she felt skittish, in fans or concertinas or crinolines. In the interstices, she placed glass beads, polished stones, draped stems of ivy, sprigs of seasonal plants, flowers, porcelain figurines.

The room itself was a triumph of refined decoration: walls were draped in cream velvet, the table legs hidden under heavy linen covers, doors concealed behind drapes of finest velvet, the windows surrounded by pleated curtains, pelmets, flounces, tie-backs, nets. Paintings of flowers, many by her, elegant sketches of appealing animals, rural scenes, china plates bearing inscriptions, portraits, commemorative mottoes in cross-stitch covered the walls.

On a series of side tables, all of which were richly swathed in choice fabrics, the food was laid out: rows of cereals in matching bowls, all filled to exactly the same height; carafes of juices in which the levels never seemed to change; plates bearing neat triangles of cheese; mathematically precise slices of ham; formal cascades of bread rolls; jam dishes with the daintiest silver spoons; sugar cubes with elegant tongs; milk jugs; stacks of bowls, plates, trays of cutlery; gleaming coffee pots; fragile china tea-pots.

It gave her great satisfaction to survey the room before the guests arrived. It was an aesthetic construct of grace, order, symmetry. As long as this room survived, the society that produced it would survive, and she would survive.

When the guests arrived, she would hover anxiously, refilling cereal bowls, straightening the lines of cheese triangles, putting the serving implements back in their ordained positions. She never said anything, but she threatened like storm clouds on a summer's day.

Most guests ate a hurried breakfast, and were glad to flee.

Yet the hotel was moderately successful, for a steady trickle of people were prepared to pay to stay in the house of a family that, so the publicity had persuaded them, was prestigious.

However, with the exception of her current suitor, guests rarely returned.

* * *

From across the meadow, the tinkling sound of a harp reached her. Such a delicate, timid instrument. Such gracious music. She looked up from her work, saw the harpist, still a child, and saw the procession of a choir from a local primary school weaving its innocent way across to the stand where they would sing a folk song, a hymn, or, if the teacher was one of that unspeakable breed who had to be 'modern' and 'relevant', some ghastly modern pop song. The crowd was growing steadily, no doubt drawn out by the fine weather, and by the music that drifted across the meadow to the town.

She had finished most of the tussie-mussie, a genteel combination of gratitude, of respect, of shared values and ideas. That was the easy part. But it dodged the question. Which rose would be at the centre? Her mind toyed with her rather vague and girlish notions of passion. She saw her sensible underwear strewn across the bedroom floor in quite unaccustomed abandon. She envisaged uncertain acts of love under a harvest moon. Then she took fright as she remembered her father's dire warnings.

While unwilling to admit it, Jane's parents had recognised that she alone kept them afloat, even modestly comfortable. Her father could still take his rods and the spaniels and go fishing, or, with a gun under his arm, set out across fields on a winter's morning. In the evenings, he could still sit in the drawing room, sipping wine, dipping into the literary classics of major European cultures, listening to the radio or to music. Her mother was still perpetually and totally ineffectually busy.

They counted on Jane. She ran the hotel, paid the bills, shopped, mended, cooked. In her little free time, she painted flowers, attended courses on table decoration and book-keeping.

Now and again a young man might call, but she was too timid to encourage her suitors. Her father, fearful for his idle comfort, warned this meek virgin about the bestial side of even the apparently most refined man. He related tales of infidelity, frustration, unnatural desires. Jane was rather perplexed by the "unnatural desires", for she was not certain that she knew what natural desires were. But she did not ask for further explanations. She took her father's word for it and founded "The Ladies' Tussie-Mussie and Floral Watercolour Society".

Prolonged and enthusiastic applause followed the end

of the performance by the children's choir. Thirty shining, innocent faces, washed and tidied as if it were a Sunday, shone, as parents, aunties, uncles, grandparents, neighbours, brothers, sisters, cousins, friends cheered for their own little Hedydd or Mair or Ceri or Geraint. For a few minutes, life seemed real again, and her virgin bosom swelled with unaccustomed longings.

Then some fifth rate television nonentity, what nowadays they call a "celebrity", leapt onto the stage, and, with over-amplified and overpaid vulgarity, announced the arrival of some local councillor. The crowds drifted away towards the ice-cream stands, towards hand-made soap and organic honey, and even towards "The Ladies' Tussie-Mussie and Floral Watercolour Society".

She had now completed the arrangement -except for the single rose for the centre. She patiently explained to visitors, perhaps even to herself, how the choice of each flower, of each blade of grass, spelled out a maiden's shy response to her admirer, how the colour of the chosen bloom would tell her lover all he needed to know.

The councillor finally finished his litany of the year's events: a new park bench, a decrease in litter, a worrying surge in dog-fouling, a new classroom, better buses. All of them, apart from the dog-fouling, were apparently directly attributable to his wise custodianship of the community.

Jane turned to her easel and brushes as if they could provide a refuge from such …. She hesitated, searching for the word. Such people were no doubt well-meaning, and, of course, it was important to have benches in the park without piles of litter all around them, but it was all so ... Trivial? Mundane? Irrelevant? Inessential? Peripheral? Yes, perhaps that was it: pompous and peripheral.

She opened her paint box which was as immaculate as everything else in her life: pans and tubes without the slightest trace of dried colour; a clean water pot; pristine sponges; brushes as soft and as clean as the day she had bought them. That was it with watercolour. It was capable of such strength and of such delicacy. There were no lumps of thick oil paint, no garishly synthetic streaks of gouache. Water colour was minimal, refined. A touch of red called up a sunset that glowed and shimmered in the vaporous heavens. The whole world could be expressed, at least all that part of the world worthy of being expressed, in a few deft touches, in the subtle spread of a drop of water. There was no need for more than that. Those who could understand would understand.

Things were a lot easier when her father died. Firstly, he was not there to fritter away the money. Secondly, she could organise the business better, without interference. When her mother died a little later, she took complete control of the estate, and worked to provide a safe if not extravagant income.

The suitor had continued to come to the hotel even after her father, his fishing companion, had died. He would sit over silent breakfasts and over afternoon tea, occasionally complimenting his hostess on the table decoration or on some slight change to the décor. At times he would mention her father, say how he was missed, although her response to these comments was muted.

He had never really noticed Jane, at least not as anything more than the quite pleasant and inoffensive daughter of the house. He had been too busy talking to her father, exchanging opinions about various flies and nymphs, picking up tips about the best spots, the likely times. Now he would idly watch her. She would straighten a cushion, adjust the fall of the curtains in their ties, move a chair a little this way or that. He saw that although she was not charming, she was predictable.

One day, as the afternoon sun streamed in through the windows, he watched her carefully re-arrange the newspapers on the table where they were placed for the guests to read. Patiently, carefully, she straightened each paper, folded them, smoothed them, flattened and squared them, so that they were almost as if they had never been read. Then she lined them up exactly in the centre of the table, each paper overlapping the next by exactly the same amount.

At that moment he realised that he should announce his intentions.

He let it be known that he was financially secure, that he was prepared to move wherever she should choose, that he would not make unwanted demands in that way.

His declaration both frightened and disappointed her.

Frightened because of her father's warnings of the ruthless ways of men. Perhaps, a trifle disappointed that he was not a lusty ravisher of maidens.

Jane had never thought of him as anything other than a guest, much like any other. Except that when he took ham or cheese from the plates, he did so in a way that retained symmetry, instead of taking whatever was closest or easiest. She had to admit that her loitering around the breakfast room was less obsessive when he was there. And when he left, and when she hurried to the table, as was her way, she would see that order had been retained. At times, he had made a slightly different, even whimsical symmetry, and almost a smile would come to her face.

She took her board in her hand and with a few bold sweeps of her largest brush, and the slightest touch of a delicate egg-shell blue paint, she applied the background wash, a slightly more intense tone at the top suggesting the sky and graduated to the merest hint of colour at the bottom where the stems would twist and form an intricate base. Then, with a fine brush, she sketched in a leaf, barely discerned against the background, a curling petal, the sweep of a stem reflecting the light on one side.

As she worked, she drew more visitors to the stand, intrigued by her skill and concentration, by the subtle intricacy of her design.

Now that she was working, not agonising over the choice of the central flower, she was more relaxed. Now she would explain, as she dabbed her brush on the paper, what this flower meant, what that stem indicated. A stem leaning to the right, she explained, means "I". To the left means "You". A flower standing upright conveys an affirmative meaning. Pointing down, it conveys the negative. A rose without thorns suggests hope. Without leaves it suggests fear.

With a few deft strokes, she created a rose stem, upright, pointing left, as yet without leaf or thorn or flower.

To another visitor she explained that the meaning of the flowers changed according to their position in the arrangement. For example, a marigold conveys pain, yet its position clarifies whether the pain is one of spiritual troubles, unrequited love, or the uneasiness of melancholy.

She turned her painting to the visitor, pointed out how the arrangement conveyed to the recipient that the creator of the tussie-mussie is moved by his tokens of esteem, is indebted for his generosity, and wishes to ....

She hesitated.

"Yes?" an attractive young couple enquired, rather caught up in this arcane world.

She explained the gamut of responses, from polite refusal to eager acceptance, from white to red.

"And a moss rose ...," she added, and then stopped.

"Yes?"

"Well, a moss rose indicates sensuality, passion, ... lust." she almost whispered.

"Now I know what to get for our anniversary," the man laughed, his fingers slipping under the light jumper, as Jane was rather perturbed to notice.

For a moment she watched them, mouth to mouth, body to body, happy, laughing, touching, whispering. Her brush hovered uncertainly, excited, afraid. Then she dipped the tip of the fine sable in a darker green and thorns appeared the length of the stem.

"Have you got a painting of a moss rose?" he asked.

A little shamefacedly, as if exhibiting some

pornographic work, Jane showed a glorious, full red rose that luxuriated wantonly on a background of tulips.

He did not haggle, did not hesitate. A few moments later, he slipped the neatly bubble-wrapped painting into a bag, and the couple walked away, laughing, arm in arm, and, Jane noticed, with hands slipping onto buttocks as they swayed across the grass.

* * *

They had never touched. At the funerals of her parents, they had shaken hands, but through gloves. She could not face the thought of certain intimacies. She shrank from certain things that she did not understand, had never experienced, and of which she did not even allow herself to think. She thought of so many private, intimate things, and recoiled before the potential violation of her neatly arranged drawers, before an unacceptable promiscuity in the linen basket. What kind of underwear did he wear? She drove this thought from her mind.

She turned away and stared down at the paint box where the paints reflected her quandary. She hesitated for a moment, then she reached for the white tube.

* * *

She did not see him again that day, or ever. He must have passed by the stand, seen the white rose, and understood. By the time she had put everything back into her car, and driven back to the hotel, he had checked out and left. She did not receive the customary card at Christmas. The next year, he did not return to the hotel.

Jane carried on as normal, attending to the hotel,

making and painting floral arrangements, and teaching others to enjoy that genteel art.

On those rare occasions, when some uncontrollable dream or a stray thought in an unguarded moment of reverie stirred her loins, she blamed something unseemly seen on television, or cheese eaten too late in the evening.

When the art and craft fair came round again the next year, she knew in advance what the tussie-mussie would be. As usual she was up early. Again she set up her careful, elegant display. For a moment, she studied the painting of last year's tussie-mussie. The flowers were as bright and as perfect as when they had been painted, the white rose as pure and unsullied as ever.

At least art survives, she thought. Whereas the real flower, that pure white rose, lay dried, withered, shrunken in tissue paper amid her coy underwear.

"O rose, who dares to name thee?
No longer roseate now, nor soft, nor sweet,
But pale, and hard, and dry, as stubblewheat,--
Kept seven years in a drawer, thy titles shame thee."

This year's tussie-mussie presented no such problem. She set about the painting with as much verve as ever, and the delicate purple bowl of a flower came to life under her brush.

"What is that?" a voice asked.

"Meadow saffron," she replied.

"I've never seen a flower like that," the man added, as if his ignorance was in any way relevant.

"Colchicum autumnale. It grows in sheltered spots, in

undisturbed, damp, cool meadows."

"And what does it mean?"

"That is quite complicated. Usually flowers bloom in spring or summer, and they announce good times to come. But the meadow saffron blooms in autumn, so it points out that the good times have already gone."

"That sounds silly."

"Perhaps. There are other ideas. For the Greeks, the flower promises rebirth and perpetual youth."

"The Greeks?"

"We call it colchicum because it comes from Colchis, a city in Greece, where they thought the flower had magical powers, could even restore youth."

"I say, look over there," the man interrupted, "genuine hand-made Welsh plastic garden gnomes."

And he hurried away.

She turned back to her painting, sighed.

"But, of course, that is only a myth."

❦ ❦ ❦

Travellers

Time favours the gods

"John," she said, "isn't this wonderful? Just look at the view."

To their left, vast, empty, scrub-covered mountains loomed. The dark mass of a nearby ridge sloped down towards them, ending in a sharp rise and then dropping sheer to a valley floor a thousand feet below. The valley was a blue sea of haze amidst darker mountains that receded, paler and paler, from green to blue to grey and even white. Here and there the darker finger of a cypress tree stood out, a jagged mass of white rocks jutted from the earth. There was the drone and buzz of a million insects flitting amongst the parched flowers of thorn and cactus, the smell of wild herbs and salt on the wind. There were ageless, black-veiled crones who, perched sideways on donkeys, urged their herds of goats and spindly sheep from one empty landscape to another with the wailing, nasal chants of songs and ancient lamentations.

As the road twisted and turned, the mountains and sea danced around them.

John changed down as he guided the car between the pot-holes and bumps.

To their right, a line of low headlands stretched out, knotted white fingers of rock that bathed in a deep blue sea, guarding in their primeval grasp coves edged by strips of pure white sand. Further off, an island floated in the haze, shaped almost like a crouching cat, with, as its head, a strange protuberance, perhaps some vast outcrop of stone, perhaps the remains of some ancient building or burial mound. He stared at it, trying to decide.

"John," she screamed and drew in her breath involuntarily.

The track turned back abruptly, seemed for a moment to lean upon the sky itself, before it veered away from the void and climbed, ever more steeply, ever upwards.

The front wheel dropped into a pot-hole and the car shuddered and slewed around. The tyres scrabbled for a hold on the dusty surface. There was the startling, thin crash of glass as a bottle rolled off the back seat and shattered on the floor. For a moment they remained balanced precariously on the very edge.

For a second he hesitated.

And then she screamed again, a long-drawn, piercing scream.

* * *

A brilliant scarab settled for a second on the windscreen, only to be swept off by the wipers. He must have turned them on in his frantic movements. and now they swept across the dust-caked screen, grating, scratching, rhythmically, insistently, like a metronome, except that the tempo would slow down, gradually, inexorably.

* * *

"Horses," he mumbled, "I can hear horses."

There was no answer.

"There's somebody coming," he said. "I can hear horses."

He crawled out of the car and stood expectantly in the road.

"There's someone coming," he called again.

He listened, but now he heard only the crackling of the insects' wings, the dry rustling of the poppies, the far-off hiss of a placid sea, the sigh of the breeze.

"I thought I heard horses," he said, surprised. "I was sure."

* * *

The dust of the track hung in the air and settled like a fine white shroud over the car -and over him. The stench of petrol and of the wine that had spilled from the broken bottle nauseated him, and so he walked a few yards along the road to escape it. He sat on a boulder and stared grimly out at the sea.

He jumped, startled, as he felt the touch of a hand on his shoulder. He span round and saw Jane staring down at him.

They sat in silence. The sun turned further round and the island out in the sea took on different forms as valleys fell into new shadows, as light picked out new crests and summits. As time wore on, the strange outcrop at one end, the cat's head, seemed even to have ears, and then again it looked more like a ruined building.

"Do you think we'd better go back?" she asked.

He stared back down the road towards the bend.

"To where we started? Just so that we can start again?"

Then, after a while, he added with a wry smile, "Perhaps he'll send his dog to show us."

She stared silently at the empty land.

"There's that noise again," he called out, and he got to his feet, "Can't you hear it? Horses."

* * *

"No problem," the car-hire man had said, "no problem. It's easy. Even my dog could find it, and he can't even find his own tail sometimes." He laughed, and the sun glinted on a gold tooth, on the right, at the top.

He reached out a foot and gently poked a large, yellow dog. The dog did not move: it raised one eyelid a little, sighed, and continued its slumber in the morning sun.

"Don't worry," he said with a vibrant confidence that could not but assuage their fears.

They seemed a race apart, these men of the island. They were too tall and slim, their skin was too brown, their moustaches curled too extravagantly, their eyes sparkled too darkly, their black hair was too shiny, too perfumed with the smoke of exotic woods and the dry tang of thyme. They were civil and polite, but their courtesy went with a smile that hinted at the wildness of the land itself. They were charming, but with a mischievous charm.

"Believe me. Don't worry." He threw back his head and laughed with childlike joy, the gold tooth flashing. "You go down past the church, up the hill in front of the school, and just keep going. It's not far. You'll be there in time to swim today."

It was already hot, and the street was alive with people busy with the business of being on holiday. Some headed for the sand where they would lie, turning over with clockwork precision, to toast and stultify in the sun. Some would stagger from bar to bar. Others scuttled about, complaining and laughing, eager to get the lowest possible price on another useless bauble.

They were going to see the real country. They had it all planned. As soon as they could get away from this man, they would be off.

He reached out, took her hand and raised it gallantly, laughingly, to his lips. A lock of shiny hair fell across her hand, smelling faintly of herbs and olive-wood.

"Enjoy your holiday. Don't worry. The sun will be here tomorrow."

She drew back, startled, shocked, afraid. His skin was too brown, the lines around his eyes too fine, the dry touch of his lips on her hand indelible.

He took John's hand in his, clasped his arm with his other hand.

"It's all right," he said, "we are not bandits. We just

like the sun and the sea, and perhaps we laugh too much. But the sun and the sea will be here tomorrow, and we won't. So you have to hurry up."

He turned and steered them towards the car, opening the door with a bow.

"Madame," he said.

She did not notice his invitation. She stood on the pavement, staring down the street.

Six large, grey horses plodded steadily towards them. They were draped in gold and silver cloths which hung almost to the ground, and which were covered with shining medals and coloured icons. As they advanced, the hollow, rhythmic beating of their hoofs was accompanied by the thin squeaking of the harnesses and by the tinkling ring of a hundred ornaments. They were pulling a low, flat platform slung between four enormous wooden wheels. At the front of this cart there was a high box on which the frail figure of the driver stood. His face was smooth and small, dark-skinned. His black eyes were half hidden by a kind of headgear of brilliant silks decorated with bindings and ribbons and sequins of all colours. He wore a large, floating shirt of crimson silk with gold brocade around the collar and cuffs. Pale pink breeches and coloured pumps peeped from underneath a swirl of bright skirts.

The car-hire man followed her gaze and his smile faded. Then he laughed again, took them both by the arm, and guided them back into his shop.

"It's the sun that does it," he laughed, by way of excuse, "I've forgotten to see your driving licence. Please," he coaxed them, "it is too hot now. Come inside where it is cooler."

As if to prove his point, he pushed the dog with his foot.

"Hey, Dog, it's too hot."

He poked the dog until it got up and plodded wearily into the shade.

"I've got to tell him everything," he laughed.

She was still watching the horses. She realized what was on the back of the cart: two coffins standing up at an angle, not quite upright, but almost so.

"But," she stammered, aghast, turning to the man and then to John, "but ..."

"But you had it just now," John protested.

"Sorry?" he asked.

"My driving licence," John complained, a little tired of this gallantry.

There were no lids on the coffins and she could see clearly the froth of coloured silks inside.

"Yes, perhaps," he faltered, "but I did not fill in the form. Just a moment. Please."

"What is it?" she asked.

"Nothing," he answered, and he virtually pushed them inside and then closed the door. "Just a funeral. People from the mountains."

"But there are two," she insisted.

"Yes," he said. "A tragedy."

"What happened?" she asked, still struck by horror, and yet still fascinated. "Were they very old?"

"Old?" he repeated with surprise, "what does that mean? You are always too young to die."

"But it's horrible," she said.

"What?"

"There are no lids," she said slowly. "And they are raised up like that, as if they were on display, as if they wanted to make us see them."

"No," he said slowly, "it is to make them see us."

"What do you mean?"

He walked over to her, took her by the arm, tightened his grip when she tried to back away.

"Come away, now," he said, "It's just our way, the way of the men of the mountains."

He led them both across the room to a large map pinned to the wall.

"They say that it is so beautiful here that many years ago this was the home of the gods. They loved the warmth of the sun and the cool of the sea, the silence of the mountains, the smell of wild herbs, the sigh of a breeze, and ..." He paused, smiled, shrugged with feigned innocence. "... perhaps I should not say this to the lady, but the men and women of the island were also very beautiful, and so there were many, many children who were part god and part human. That is why, so they say, the people of the island are as they are today." And he drew himself up to his full height, smiled extravagantly and bowed.

"And what about the driving licence?" John interrupted, anxious to be on his way, tired of the swaggering prattle.

"That doesn't explain why they don't close the coffins," Jane persisted.

"It's their last chance to see the sea, to feel the sun, to smell the herbs on the mountain-side, to hear the birds and to taste the salt on the breeze, and the men of the mountains believe that, if they are gods, their souls will wake up and go back to the mountains to live there forever. And that is why they cannot close the coffins."

"Come now," he continued, "let me show you the road you must take."

As he spoke, the horses could be seen through the window at the other end of the room.

"Come. Don't worry." He turned again to the map. "It's just their way. Here. You see, it is easy. Past the church, up the hill and you keep on this road. You can't go wrong."

"But," she asked hesitantly, "they don't bury them like that, do they?"

He shrugged his shoulders.

Their words were drowned by the heavy thud of the horses' hoofs, the wheels, the clinking of the ornaments that hung everywhere. They could see only the base of the cart and of the stand against which the coffins leaned.

One mourner walked behind the cart. He was tall and slim, dressed in black, his features hidden in the shadow of a wide-brimmed hat, under which only a long, curling moustache could be seen.

The mourner turned, caught her stare. For a moment he seemed surprised. Then he lifted his hat. There was the slightest inclination of the head and a flashing smile.

"But ..." she stammered.

The man shrugged as if to say it was not his fault.

"A cousin," he said apologetically, and he waved discreetly to the mourner. "From the mountains."

He signalled to the mourner to move on. Then he turned back, smiling, a more urgent tone in his voice.

"You go now. You go. Enjoy yourselves."

"But he's just like you," she said.

"Do you think?" he asked. "Some people do say there is a resemblance."

"A resemblance!" she insisted, turning to stare quite unashamedly at the mourner, "he is your double. He even has ..." And her hand went to her mouth.

"It's all right," he said, and he smiled and the gold tooth seemed to flash even more ostentatiously. "Some people say it is lucky, say it is because we are descended from gods that we can carry the sun with us in our mouths."

"But you go now," he said. "You go or you miss the chance to swim."

"And what about the licence?" John asked.

"Licence? What licence?"

"The driving licence!"

"Oh, don't worry. You go now. Hurry."

* * *

"I can't hear anything," she said.

No horse appeared. He sank back down on the rock.

"I was sure," he said. "And a tinkling sound."

They stared at the impassive, empty land.

"It isn't an island at all," he said, almost to himself.

"What?"

"Out there with the strange shape on the end. I thought it was an island, but it is a headland. There's a strip of land running between the hills."

Jane did not seem particularly interested or impressed.

"What are we going to do?" she asked.

"I don't know," he mumbled. "I don't know how far we can get with the car. If it will go at all. Well, we said we wanted something different, to see the real thing. So here it is. You can't get more real than being lost in the middle of nowhere, with not another soul for miles."

He spread his arms wide to indicate the vast, unresponsive landscape, turned his face to the heavens and shouted at the top of his voice.

"Hello, can anybody hear me?" He turned towards her again, "You see? Nobody!"

He picked up a stone and hurled it at a large boulder at the side of the road. The stone bounced off, and there was the noise of breaking glass as it fell among the weeds.

He went over to where the stone had landed, on the very edge of the road where the hill fell away almost vertically, a tangled jumble of rocks and patches of white, dusty earth where great fleshy plants grew, like fat green fingers edged with brilliant purple flowers. A lizard sat on a stone, stared at him with head cocked to one side.

"John," she called.

"Come and look at this," he called, bending down to pick up a large box that he had found among the weeds.

"John," she called, "come away from the edge. Please." Her voice had broken.

He smiled, and then turned back towards her.

It was a rectangular metal box, with one glass side that the stone had smashed. The glass was so caked with dirt that he could not see inside, but the box rattled when he shook it.

He twisted back the rusty lid, to find, to his disappointment, that there was no horde of ancient gold inside. Just a few shards of coloured pottery, a cheap, glass bottle, and a sheet of thin metal on which a picture had been stamped. It seemed, he noted with distaste, vaguely religious, showing a smiling face with some kind of crown and a long moustache. It must also have been brightly coloured once, for, in the deeper folds, flakes of colour still remained: a crease of red on the robe, jewels of green and blue on the crown, a dash of blood in the lips, and a patch of gold on the teeth.

"It reminds me of something," she said.

They stared at the picture for a moment, and then she said, "We've got to do something. We can't just sit here and wait."

But they sat on the rock, unable to decide.

Why had they not been content to stay with the hordes? No thirst for knowledge and understanding stopped them slowly roasting like spitted animals on a swarming beach, and sinking into oblivion in nightly stupor.

So much effort, so much planning for so little! To end up like this! It should have been worth it. Things always seem worth it, in advance, otherwise you wouldn't bother in the first place. But then things rarely turn out as you plan.

He made as if to hurl the box down the hill.

"No. No, don't," she said, "put it back. Perhaps somebody has lost it."

"But it's been there for years," he said. "It's almost rusted away."

"Never mind," she said. "You don't know. Just put it back."

He shrugged and walked back to the boulder where he had found it. He stopped short in surprise.

Immediately past the boulder, hidden over the lip of the road, a track led down the hill side. It was narrow, but it did not seem that much worse than the road on which they had travelled.

"Jane," he called, as if this might somehow solve their problem, "come here. Quick."

Of course it didn't solve anything. It really made things worse, for now they had three things to choose from, instead of just two.

The map was not much use, for it showed only one

red line from A to B, from the town where they had hired the car to the village where they had booked their hotel. Just one bold, unwavering line, which, as they had discovered to their cost, was a deceitfully optimistic description of this miserable track.

The only thing, he advised, was to approach the situation rationally, calmly.

Firstly, there was little reason to try to go back. They were sure that they had taken the right road, and as there was only one road, then they had to be on the right road now. That was logical.

Secondly, they had to be almost there. He would have thought that they should have arrived already. But then again, 70 miles on a broken, rutted track that clambered over the mountains, that dropped vertiginously down to the sea, and then struggled upwards over the next rise, 70 miles like that could take for ever.

Conclusion: they were on the right road and couldn't be too far away.

And that left only one remaining problem: which road should they take?

Now a road is a main road because lots of people use it, because it goes a long way. But a side road doesn't go far, so there had to be something quite close down the smaller track. That was also logical.

They decided to try the track. Besides, if they were going to get lost, it was better to get lost close to the sea, so that they would always have some idea of where they were. Once you were in the mountains, you could go round and round forever.

The car limped down the steep track which twisted and turned as it threaded a tortuous course between rocks and ravines. At one point they crossed a small bridge across a rushing stream, whose clear, running water was strangely out of place in this barren landscape. The track turned and followed the stream down a narrow gorge between the mountains. The sea had disappeared from sight, even though he could not work out how that was possible, for it had appeared so close from the road. Yet as long as they followed the stream, they had to be going in the right direction, downhill, closer to the sea.

A little later the narrow gorge widened out, and rows of enormous, deciduous trees lined the road. There was no sun down between the high walls of the gorge, and a thin drifting mist hung over the stream and between the trees, floating over the meadows beyond. They felt suddenly cold and shivered in their thin summer clothes. Jane moved closer, and they held hands, neither mentioning the apprehension they felt. At times, the mist thickened and obscured the valley ahead.

"I'm sorry," he said.

She did not answer, but tightened her hold.

They seemed to have been going for ages, increasingly convinced that they had made the wrong choice, when the track widened and they came back out into brilliant sunlight. The valley was much wider, with rows of olive trees stretching off into the distance, their twisted, pock-ridden trunks like nightmare creatures holding up the light canopy of green and silver. At the feet of the trees, circles of green grass huddled in the shade, a vivid contrast to the parched yellow around them. The stream now flowed peacefully along its pebbled bed.

"We must be almost there," he said.

The road turned and ran alongside a strip of sand next to the sea. A couple of boats, brightly painted in a turquoise that was almost identical to the colour of the water, rocked lazily a few yards off-shore. To their left there was a field, perhaps an orchard, with orderly rows of trees underneath which was a blaze of poppies and daisies. Donkeys and goats grazed quietly, their bells tinkling gently as they moved between the trees.

"Is this it?" she asked.

About eighty yards ahead of them there were a few tumble-down buildings clustered around a jetty that ran out into the sea. In front of the buildings there was a courtyard, or at least a kind of clearing amongst the trees, where tables and chairs were set out.

Right in the middle of the courtyard was a large dog, sprawled out in the dust, apparently fast asleep in the sun.

They walked slowly towards the buildings, apprehensively.

As they approached, the dog slowly opened one eye and surveyed them.

"Do you think this can be it?" she asked.

"It can't be," he said.

This was certainly not their luxury hotel, complete with swimming pools, water sports, three restaurants, tennis courts and extensive gardens. Nor was it the charming village that offered every facility to the discerning traveller.

"We'll have to ask."

* * *

"Hello," a voice greeted them warmly from the doorway. "How nice to see you. Come in, sit down, please."

From out of the shadow a man stepped. He was tall and lean, with long, black hair and a drooping moustache that curled around his lips. He stood aside, stretched out his arm to invite them to enter, bowed and smiled. There was a glimmer of gold in the shadow.

"Come in, please," he urged again. "It is all ready. We are expecting you."

"I think you're making a mistake," John explained. "We just want to ask our way. We are lost. We are not coming here."

"I am sorry," the man said with a patient smile, "I should have said that we are always expecting travellers. That is our business."

John went to step forward, but Jane dug her fingers deep into his flesh.

"Let's go," she said urgently, and she pulled at his arm.

"Please," he encouraged them, "would you like a nice, cool drink? It is a hot day."

"Of course," he said, changing the subject diplomatically, "you may sit out here if you prefer. It is very pleasant now in the shade of the trees." He turned quickly back to the door and called out "Maria, Maria!"

Then he picked up an apron made of some coarse, striped material and tied it around his waist. He took a cloth and hurried to sweep a few crumbs from a table and to dust the seats of two chairs.

"Please," he said, "Please to sit down. You must be tired."

"It's him," Jane whispered.

"Maria," he called again, "Maria."

A slight figure swathed in brilliantly coloured silks appeared. She crossed the courtyard, the rustle of her clothes mingling with the sighing of the breeze in the leaves overhead. She wore a loose blouse which was covered in intricate embroidery, long, full skirts edged with elaborate brocades, and a silk scarf wound around her head, covering everything except her smooth, dark face, and her white, regular teeth.

She spread a cloth on the table and put two glasses and a pitcher of iced lemon juice on it. She turned, smiled, and went back to the building with the faintest whisper of silks.

"It's him," Jane insisted.

"Please, I'm sorry," he said, and hurried forwards, still misunderstanding her reluctance. The ice chinked tantalizingly as he poured. "Please. Then you will feel better."

"We had a bit of trouble with the car," John started.

"I am sorry," he said. "Please, please," he urged as he pushed the lemon juice towards them. "It's very good.

Drink."

"We must have hit a bump," John lied.

"Our roads are so bad," he consoled them.

"It is you, isn't it?" Jane suddenly blurted out, her anger dominating her apprehension. "It is you, so why are you pretending not to recognize us?"

He looked at her blankly, as if totally confused by her questions.

"It is you," she maintained. "You hired us the car this morning. In town."

He glanced round to look for some explanation, but John was also staring at him suspiciously.

"I am sorry," he said with a smile in which the gold tooth seemed downright provocation, "I am sorry but I don't understand."

"Well what about funerals?" she demanded aggressively. "Have you been to any funerals today?"

He shrugged, hands spread out, palms upturned, smiling tolerantly.

"No?" she shouted, almost crying with fear and anger and frustration, "No funerals? No car hire? Perhaps you have a cousin descended from the gods?"

"Cousins?" he repeated quizzically, as if grasping at something that he had understood, "yes, I have many cousins. But I don't see ..."

He stopped, looked at her more carefully. Then he continued in a brighter, more confident voice, turning to John for support and confirmation.

"Perhaps you would like to rest," he suggested

tactfully. "It has been very hot, and you have had many problems. But now you are here. Everything is all right and I take care of you."

He turned, clapped his hands, called out quickly, "Maria! Maria!"

John was about to demur diplomatically.

"No," Jane shouted, "we are not coming here. We are going to ...."

She stopped because she could not remember the name.

"As I said, we are rather lost," John said apologetically.

* * *

Perhaps they should have left. Perhaps they should have pushed on. But they couldn't. They weren't even on the right road, the man told them, and there was no telephone, and the car was not good and they could not have walked all the way back up to the main road and then on to the hotel.

But, he said with a smile, as if sorry that he could do no more, he would take the vouchers for the other hotel, sort it all out for them.

So they followed as he led them into the courtyard and then up a white-washed staircase with railings painted in a delicate aquamarine. The room was large, cool, clean and light, with a second door giving out onto a balcony that overlooked the sea and from which a small, rather rickety staircase, led down to the beach.

They walked to while away their time, to try and

beguile themselves, but they could not be free of their anger. Their day was lost! Lost beyond recall!

They were so caught up that they did not notice the warmth of the sand between their toes as they walked barefoot along the beach, or see the sun set beyond the far-off headland, across the sea that was almost black with light. They did not hear the gentle clink of bells as donkeys nuzzled each other in the olive groves, or as goats bleated, lying lazily amidst head-high flowers. He did look up and turn round when he heard the insistent whinny of a horse, but he could not see it. For a few moments, several ducks followed them, chattering expectantly, before they waddled away, disappointed, to attend to more legitimate business. The dog even raised its head, its tail even stirred, but as they stalked along, it went back to sleep again.

Then they pored over their maps, made out their lists, re-arranged all their plans. As they did so, Maria silently set before them plates of food that they toyed with mechanically. She poured chilled, white wine from a dark bottle that they sipped unthinkingly.

It wasn't because this was a broken-down hotel on a deserted beach in the middle of nowhere that they were so angry. They didn't need the swimming-pools, the saunas, the jacuzzis, the tennis courts, the elegant bars and accomplished waiters, the surf-boards, the golden-haired, long-legged, naked bodies sprawled on glistening sands. Even though, of course, they had paid for all of that. It was the real things they wanted to see: the ruined temples and forgotten villages, the flower-edged roads and picturesque hamlets where handsome urchins follow you, laughing and shouting, through wisteria-draped alleys; the museums and galleries where you can discover the glory of a culture that used to be and was no more, but which might still, across the ages, whisper cryptic clues to the secret of a better way of being; the ruined palaces of mythical kings where men fought with monsters, spoke to Gods, and savoured ineffable delights with olive-skinned virgins.

"You like?" he asked, as, unheeding, they finished the meal.

"Oh, yes," said John quickly, "very nice, thank you."

Jane glowered.

"You are very busy," he said, glancing at the papers on the table.

"Yes," John said, "we are planning our holiday. We want to see it all."

"What do you want to see?" he asked. "I can tell you what is good."

"Thank you very much," Jane said sharply, "we have it all organized. We have a book."

"Ah. A book," he said. Just for a second his smile faded. But then he laughed and the gold tooth flashed, and he poured them all a glass of wine.

"To books!" he laughed and raised his glass.

"Yes," John explained, "we want to see the temples."

"The temples," he laughed. "Very good. Does your book tell you of our temple?"

He took John by the arm and led him out to the terrace behind the buildings.

"Look," he said, pointing out across the moonlit sea.

The headland that they had seen earlier curled out around the bay. The strange bump which had looked like a cat's head, had taken on a different shape now: a jagged mass silhouetted against the light, night sky.

"And what is that temple dedicated to?" John asked, not entirely convinced.

The man turned to him, a look of surprise on his face. "Why," he said, "all temples are dedicated to the same thing! Doesn't your book tell you that?"

* * *

"And just what are they dedicated to, according to him?" Jane asked derisively as they got ready for bed.

"I didn't ask," John replied.

The touch of the cool sheets might have calmed them, but they remained apart, curled up tightly on opposite sides of the bed, as they tried to find sleep to escape their unresolved clouds of anger and pain.

But he found sleep elusive.

He turned over, only to sense the hard hostility of her back curled up against him.

"I can't sleep," he said. There was no answer.

He got up slowly, silently and went out onto the balcony. The air was warm as he stepped outside, and he tiptoed gingerly down the staircase.

He sat for a long time on the bottom step, staring out across the beach to the sea that rose and fell gently like a sleeping giant, its crests glittering in a pale light. He tried to distinguish the lines of a temple in the shapeless pile on the headland, but could not do so convincingly.

He sat and listened to the whisperings of his unhappiness sighing in time, like a familiar pain, with the sea and the breeze.

He looked up suddenly and shivered. He must have been slumbering, for the moon had disappeared, and the sea was faintly luminescent under a dark sky. He turned round in surprise, for he had heard a horse whinny, and then suddenly there was the noise of hoofs, a dull, resonant sound as they thundered in the soft sand. The noise approached quickly from the left, and he caught a brief glimpse of a large grey horse as it crossed in front of him, silhouetted against the sea, mane and tail flying. Then the rider suddenly checked the horse, and turned. They moved slowly towards him.

At first he could make out only a head leaning round the neck of the horse to peer in his direction. Then he heard the musical sound of a thin, liquid laugh. The rider stood up in the stirrups, twisted round on the horse's back, raising an arm in greeting, and he saw the naked, full body of a woman, her head thrown back as she laughed and waved, perched high on the horse's back. She leaned forward and stretched out her hand to him.

He huddled back into the shadows, afraid. After a moment, she turned again, grasped the reins and raced away, her high laughter trailing behind her as she disappeared into the darkness. From somewhere in the dark, a deep, ringing laugh replied.

He stood and peered into the darkness which had

swallowed up the horse and rider until his eyes watered, and a slight chill made him shudder. Then he got up and climbed back up the staircase.

As he got to the balcony, he heard laughter and he glimpsed a shape moving in the darkness.

"Hello," the shape called out, "did you have a nice walk? It is a lovely night for dreaming, isn't it?"

He saw the man closing the door from his bedroom and stepping back onto the balcony.

"I am just looking for you," he continued. "Your car is fixed tomorrow morning."

John walked up to him, stared at the door, the handle of which the man was still holding.

"What?" John demanded uncertainly, "How?"

"Maria," he answered. "I sent Maria on the horse. Didn't you see her go? Didn't she say hello to you?"

"Maria," he repeated quietly.

He felt sweat form on his brow and run down to the tip of his nose, so that as he tried to control himself, he was plagued by this irritating itch as the bead of sweat hung precariously.

"But," John questioned, his eyes fixed on the swarthy hand that still rested on the handle, "why are you looking here if you knew I was outside?"

"It is hot tonight," the man laughed. "Too hot to sleep. But the breeze is coming, and it will be better. You sleep now, and everything will be good tomorrow."

"But ..." John insisted, and he pushed open the door a little to glance inside. Then he turned back, but the man had gone. From the staircase he heard a deep laugh.

"You sleep now," he called out.

John hesitated, uncertain. Then he pushed open the bedroom door and went in.

Jane slept, curled up even tighter. As he slipped into bed, he felt the hard ridge of her spine against him. For a moment she stirred, asked if he was well.

"I can't sleep," he replied. "I went outside for a moment."

"Oh," she mumbled drowsily, and then suddenly she trembled. "I had the strangest dream," she continued, pulling herself tighter, "I dreamt that that man ..." And she fell back asleep, her knees almost touching her chin.

* * *

They were awakened by the sunlight pouring into their room, and by the sound of someone singing outside. When they went downstairs, they found the man busy with his chores.

"Good morning," he cried out, "did you have a good sleep? You feeling better now?"

"Thank you," John muttered coolly, and he walked over to the door. The car stood outside.

"And you, lady," he asked with a smile that made the gold tooth flash in the sombre room, "you sleep well too?"

She did not answer, but stared at him as if she was trying to remember something.

"A beautiful day," he said. "Just right to swim. You go

to swim?" he asked.

"And what did they say about the car?" John asked as he turned back from the door.

"The car? Nothing," he shrugged. "It's O.K.. No bill."

"So we'll go then," Jane stated.

"Don't you want to swim?" he asked with surprise. "Don't you want to visit the temple? I thought you wanted to visit temples. It is the most beautiful one," and then he added with perhaps a little irony, "even if it is not in your book."

"If you would just show us the road on the map," John answered.

"Maps! Books! You must be careful," he said. "They do not say everything, and sometimes they are very hard to read, to understand what they tell you."

They looked at him quite scornfully and smiled thinly.

John took the map from the car and spread it out on the bonnet.

The man shrugged, conceding defeat.

"If you have to go," he said. Then he laughed, the sun glinting on the gold tooth, making him look quite dashing. "If you have to go!"

He leaned over the map next to them, a faint smell coming from his hair as he brushed past them, a faint, dry smell.

Jane shuddered a little and drew back.

"No problem," he said, "no problem. It's easy. Even ..."

"Even your dog could find it, I suppose," Jane

interrupted acidly, sure that now she had proof.

"I am sorry?" he asked.

"No problem," she almost spat out in reply, "it's easy. You were going to say that even your dog could find it."

He stared at her in bewilderment.

"I say it's easy, even though the road is not good, and maps are hard to understand," he replied. "I'm sorry. I do not understand."

"No," she said, "I suppose you don't." She turned and started to move away, but then she turned back. "Forget it!" she said. "It's a joke."

"I see," he laughed, "a joke! Very good! I remember that. Even my dog could find it!"

He turned back to John, still laughing, and clapped him on the shoulder. "Come, my friend, I show you."

"This is the town," he said, irritating John by his patience, by talking to him as if he were a child, "and this is where you want to go. Yes?"

"Yes," John answered impatiently.

"And this is the road," and his long, brown finger followed the red line that snaked across the paper. "And this is where you turned off yesterday."

John stared at the map in disbelief. A thin, twisting line turned off the main road about halfway along, weaving its way down a valley to the sea.

He snatched the map up to study it more closely. The road was marked quite clearly.

"It is not possible," he said, turning the map over and

over to examine it. "It is not possible. The road was not marked yesterday."

The man shrugged, as if lost for words. John took the map over to Jane, showed it to her, had it confirmed that no turning had been on the map. They couldn't both have been that stupid! It was not possible.

"It is not the same map," he argued. "It is not possible."

"Maps," the man said humbly, "Maps are like books, or even temples: they are easy to read only if you understand what they are saying."

"No," John shouted, "it is not possible."

Then, and before she could escape, the man took her hand and raised it to his lips. A lock of hair fell forward, smelling faintly of herbs and olive-wood. The touch of his lips shocked her, angered her, bemused her.

* * *

They set off in silence back along the road they had taken the previous evening. As they were about to turn away from the sea, back up the narrow valley, he caught a glimpse in his rear-view mirror of horses galloping along the sand. The beat of the hoofs throbbed in his ears, and he turned to see better, to see if there was a rider clinging to one of them, but a sharp cry called his attention back to the road and to the bend ahead.

"What's wrong with you?" she asked. "Once is enough, isn't it? What are you looking at?"

She turned round, but saw nothing except the sea and the sand and the cliffs already closing around the village.

"Nothing," he said. "Just the sea."

But he could still hear the pounding of the hoofs, that exhilarating, primitive whinny of the horse, and high-pitched cascades of laughter.

Soon they came out at the junction, and swung right, turning back onto the main road to continue their journey.

They drove on in silence into the empty mountains. From time to time they passed through a village, a huddled jumble of white cubes with doors and window frames in violent blues and crimsons, or in the palest turquoise and faded madder. Shaded alleys twisted away, scented with orange blossom and thyme, as silent as a dream. Once they glimpsed a black-veiled shape, a wrinkled, puckered face that stared out through expressionless, opaque eyes. Once they saw an immensely tall man in riding boots, brown breeches and a green jacket and with enormous, curling moustaches. He stared at them for a moment, and then he turned and strode down a shaded alley. Once they heard a donkey bray.

Real travellers, he thought to himself with renewed confidence as he drove along the flank of a vast, bare hill side, real travellers find something more, the authentic, the essential, that which allows them to know where they are, who they are.

Shallow minds, he thought, settle for the superficial, for the trite caricature. They even rush to embrace it, over-joyed by a packaged tour of postcard landmarks and well-worn itineraries, of clichés trotted out by ignorant and venal guides, of uniformity, of predictability: same food, same bed, same thoughts, same cheap pleasures, same futility, same alive, same dead.

The road curved along the side of the mountain. It turned slightly to the right, climbed over a shoulder and dropped away a little. Suddenly the panorama spread out before them. In front there lay the sea, shimmering in the hot, brilliant light. To left and right lay the hills, bluish in the distance, a drab green in the foreground where low plants curled their leaves away from the sun, but spread out their flowers like insatiable slatterns in some pagan saga. The landscape was vast -untouched since time began, apart from the thin white line of the track that crept across it.

He pulled the car to the side of the road and stopped. The silence was a pleasure. He got out and stretched, surveying the scene in front with an almost sensuous enjoyment.

"Come and look at this, Jane," he called out.

She got out of the car and walked over to him. He slipped his arm around her waist and held her close as they stared out at the vast scene in front of them.

"And not a tourist in sight," he added.

And he breathed deeply of the dry, perfumed air. This day was rather better, and soon they would arrive.

"John," she asked hesitantly, "what's that over there?"

She pointed a few yards up the road. At the edge of the road, where the mountainside fell steeply away, there was a small shrine. A rusty metal stake supported a rectangular box with a glass front. Inside the case, an old chipped saucer, which had a rather gaudy design of reds and greens, held the remains of a burned-out candle and a few spent matches. An old bottle, half full of yellowed water, stood in one corner, with the rotted remains of a few stems caked onto its neck. At the back of the case, a religious picture of quite awful taste stood. It was very badly drawn and crudely painted, a smirking face with a long, drooping moustache with crimson lips, silver cheeks, gold teeth, and a crown of brilliant trinkets. It was framed in a flimsy surround of tarnished tin, and the face stared out at them with an air of supreme and cretinous indifference, peering smugly through the strands of a cobweb in the corner of which a large, black spider lurked attentively.

"It reminds me of something," Jane said quietly.

John looked more attentively at the ugly, garish monument.

"It's like those things on the horses at that funeral we saw yesterday. It's just the same."

"No, that's not it," she said thoughtfully. "I've seen this shrine before." She hesitated for a moment. "It's the same one," she finally mumbled to herself, as if trying to grasp something that eluded her. She turned and walked a little down the road.

"Be careful," he called out, "there's somebody coming." And he heard the hoof-beats pounding the baked earth. "Be careful. There are horses."

But no horse appeared.

"And this?" she called tremulously.

She was standing by a large rock at the side of the road, pointing to her right. When he got to her side he saw a narrow track leading away down the hill in the direction of the sea.

"What?"

"The track! This is where we were yesterday."

He looked at her in amazement.

"We're nowhere near there. What's wrong with you?"

"It's the same place," she insisted. "This is where we were yesterday."

Mountains, sea, cliffs edged with foam: it did all look similar and it would be easy to make a mistake.

"Let's go back," she said quietly.

"Back? Back where?"

"Home. Let's go home."

He sighed impatiently.

"We must be almost there now. Come on. Don't be so silly."

Although he put his arms around her and tried to shake her out of her strange mood, he could not do so.

"And isn't that his so-called temple?" she asked, pointing out to sea.

To their left a long headland stuck its finger out into the sea, low and flat at first and then suddenly rising into a hill on top of which there appeared to be some kind of ruin.

"It's nothing like it," he said exasperatedly. "It can't be. We've been driving all day. We're miles away. What's wrong with you?"

"Well, I've seen it before," she answered obstinately.

There was indeed only one way to settle it.

The car bounced and jolted down the narrow track, from rut to hole to ridge to bump until he careered around one bend and braked as hard as he could. The car skidded a little and came to a stop across the road in a blinding and suffocating cloud of white dust.

When the dust settled he stared blankly ahead. To the right there was a strip of sand next to the sea. A couple of brightly painted turquoise boats bobbed gently a few yards off-shore. To their left donkeys and goats grazed quietly, their bells tinkling gently as they moved between the olive trees. He stared in disbelief at the few buildings that huddled together at the end of the jetty. In the middle of the road, a large yellow dog, which had been fast asleep in the sun, opened one eye and stared at them. Its tail wagged lazily in the dust, and then it closed its eye and went peacefully back to sleep.

"It can't be. It's not possible," he gasped.

He snatched the map from the seat beside him. It was not possible. They had left the village, turned right, followed the same road without turning off anywhere. It was not possible to come back to the same spot in the opposite direction.

"And there are no turnings," he said aloud, answering his own objections.

He strode determinedly towards the door.

"Hello," a voice greeted him warmly from the doorway, "how nice to see you. Come in, sit down, please."

From out of the shadow a man stepped. He was tall

and lean, with long, black hair and a drooping moustache that curled around his lips. He stood aside, stretched out his arm to invite him to enter, bowed and smiled. There was a dull glimmer of gold in the shadow.

"Please," he encouraged, "would you like a nice, cool drink? It has been a hot day."

Then he picked up an apron made of some coarse, striped material and tied it around his waist. He took a cloth and hurried to sweep a few crumbs from a table and to dust the seats of two chairs.

John turned and marched back over to the car.

"It is not possible," he said, and spread the map out on the bonnet of the car.

As he was staring at it, angry and confused, he became aware of that smell of herbs and then a brown finger was placed on the map.

"Perhaps it's here you went wrong," the man said, indicating a spot on the map where the road divided. He laughed and his gold tooth flashed rakishly. "You stay with me tonight. It is all ready. Come. Please."

John stood absolutely still, staring grimly at the map, turning it over and over, looking for something that would give the game away. It was just not possible. He could feel his head swimming, his reason giving way. He had looked at the map a hundred times. There had been no turning.

"Of course," he said, "you may sit out here if you prefer. It is very pleasant now in the shade of the trees."

John span round to confront him. This charade could

not continue. He had to know. He would know, one way or another.

The man had turned back to the house and he called out "Maria, Maria."

John heard a pounding in his head like that of hoofs, and saw the child appear in the doorway. He suddenly felt tired and defeated.

He turned to Jane, and saw that she felt the same. An air of resignation and of weariness was expressed in her face.

It was too late to try to find their way out of these mountains again that evening. The next day would have to do.

Maria brought a pitcher of iced lemon juice. She smiled at them, and as she poured, a mass of fine gold bangles slipped from under the lace cuff of her sleeve and jangled at her wrist, a noise only slightly less faint than the clinking of the ice in their glasses.

The sun had already started to decline when they came out of their room to walk along the sand, and there was a haze over the horizon. The sea seemed to be of one piece, as if it had been anointed with some precious oils that lay upon its face: its surface was unbroken by any wave, and seemed to gleam like a sheet of silk that rose and fell slowly with a regular, smooth swell. In this light, the pile of stones out on the headland did seem to be more like a temple, and you could almost pick out the remains of pillars and of the pediment.

If, they imagined, if they had got to their hotel, they would have been able to swim in such a sea, be carried by this salty water, borne up in its warm embrace. They would have lain on the sand, their tensions washed away, their angers evaporating like the salt on their arms, leaving perhaps a barely discernible crust that tasted so good when they kissed.

If!

The sun dipped behind the headland, and waves began to break the surface of the water as once more it was pulled asunder by its unknown cosmic masters.

They sat to eat under the trees, served with silent grace by Maria. Small, salty fish in oil and with aromatic leaves that tasted of lemon. Pieces of lamb grilled over a wood fire, vegetables that they could not recognize, large and fleshy, but crisp and dry in the mouth, just pleasantly short of being bitter. A thin, white wine. Fruit, nuts and honey.

It was, they had to concede, albeit unconsciously, quite good. They sat in the twilight, with nightingales whistling endlessly above their heads. The animals shuffled fussily as they prepared for their sleep; flowers opened even wider as they grasped greedily at the moisture in the cooler air, spreading their perfumes to entrance the dancing insects. The dog paddled in from the road and lay quietly at their feet.

They undressed by the light of the moon and sought comfort in the coolness of the bed and the unthinking peace of sleep. He sat, leaning against the pillows, his arm around his wife who nestled against him for a while. But then she turned away, curled up and he heard her sob gently. He touched her shoulder, but she curled up more tightly from him, and he withdrew his hand. Slowly her cries subsided and at length she drifted into sleep, huddled in her private misery.

He walked slowly along the beach next to the lapping water. The moon shone quite brightly and in the water he could vaguely make out shimmering, phosphorescent shapes.

From behind him he heard the horse approaching, cantering skittishly on the hard sand. He did not, would not turn to look.

The noise of the hoofs decreased, but he could hear, feel the heavy, snorting breath upon his shoulder, smell the mysterious, pervasive musk. The horse moved alongside and he heard a high childish peal of laughter and saw the naked leg beside him. He turned, wanting to look, afraid to see. Maria sat high and straight upon the horse, laughing, smiling, an arm outstretched towards him.

He turned away, his mind scorched by her nakedness.

"Come."

He heard the whispered word.

The horse checked its stride, whinnied, this piercing, fearful noise evoking some deep atavistic terror and excitement in his being. She pulled on the reins to hold the horse in check and her thigh brushed against his arm.

He turned again.

"Come," she whispered, although her smile did not change.

He hesitated, and then looked questioningly at the horse. She held out her hand, took her foot from the stirrup.

He sat timidly behind her, uncertain of himself and of

the horse.

"Hold on," she laughed, "otherwise you will fall."

His hands hovered, wavered, tried to grip the rear of the saddle.

She laughed again, a high-pitched, rolling peal of joy against the throb of the sea.

"You better hold on," she said, "or you will fall."

His hands fluttered like the wings of a moth circling around a flame. They settled for a brief moment on the flesh. The warm, soft swell of her hips burned him as surely as any flame, scorched through his body to his mind which stumbled, swaying on the brink of the abyss, staggered drunkenly on a dangerous path.

The horse whinnied and reared a little, and then it darted forward across the sand. Her naked body pulsed with life, and she threw back her head and laughed, the wind pulling at the cascades of sound and at her black hair which streamed behind her, winding itself like some fine, perfumed web around him. His mind teetered, and then, as his grip involuntarily tightened, fell.

He heard only confusedly the strangely primitive calls as the horse ran into the night.

As he was climbing the stairs to their room, he heard deep laughter, but he saw nobody, and thought it was no doubt the sounds of Maria and the horse which still throbbed in his mind.

"John?" she called, stirring in her fitful sleep.

He made his way over to the bed, fumbling in the dimness. The covers had been pushed aside and she lay, naked and spread-eagled, across the bed. For a moment he gazed at the body that he knew so well, and yet could not know entirely. In the darkness, its paleness seemed to glow, smoothing and rounding its forms, giving a weight and volume to it that was not apparent in the bleak light of day.

As he gazed, she stirred, reached out an arm across the bed.

"John," she murmured. When she failed to find his body beside hers, she stirred more restlessly.

"John?" she called again.

"You're cold," she mumbled, and huddled up against him.

"I couldn't sleep," he said. "I went for a walk."

She turned, her eyes wide open.

"A walk? You've been for a walk?" she asked urgently.

"Just to the beach," he said, "I couldn't sleep."

"But you can't have," she mumbled sleepily.

She curled up even tighter against him, her arms clasped tightly about him in a way she had not held him for years, since they were young.

"I didn't hear you," she murmured peacefully as she drifted back to sleep. "I didn't know you had gone." And her lips began to part as her breathing became heavier, and then she smiled and pulled him close. "I had the strangest dreams," she said, and sighed.

"Sleep," he comforted, and slipped his arm around her. "Sleep now."

A smile broke across her face as she pulled closer to his body.

"I had the strangest dreams," she said, and, smiling, fell back to sleep.

* * *

"But why don't you stay," he asked, leaning over the table towards them. That faint smell of herbs drifted from his hair and his body, mingled with the nutty smell of olive wood that exuded from his skin. The smell caught in her throat, too rich, too cloying, and she coughed and shivered and pulled herself away.

"We have to go," she answered drily. "You have been very kind to us," and a cold smile forced its way to her lips.

"But don't you want to swim? Don't you want to visit the temple? Do you want a room with telephone and television?" he asked incredulously.

He smiled, leaned closer and whispered gently. "Is it not better to walk hand in hand like lovers in the night along my beach? Is it not better to gallop wildly through the moonlit waves, timidly holding another in a long embrace?"

He turned to John, and smiled with such apparent meaning that John blushed, turned away so that Jane should not see, or wonder why.

"Is it not better to lie in a cool bed and feel the touch of a lover's hand, smell the herbs of the earth, taste the crust of salt on brown skin, deeply inhale the smoke of fires, of incense and of olive wood?"

And he turned to Jane, and smiled, a smile that burned into her until she felt naked. She turned away from

John so that he should not see, and also from herself, so that she also should not see the smile that tickled the corners of her lips.

"No. It's very kind, and we are very grateful," John blustered, "but we must go. We have many things to do."

"If you have to go," he said resignedly, "if you have to go ..." And he shrugged. Then he took Jane's hand and carried it to his lips. The slight brush of his lips upon her hand shocked her, burned into her, left an indelible mark, and the faintest smell of thyme.

* * *

He drove steadily along the track alongside the beach. He slowed a little as he passed an olive grove in which a large grey horse quietly lay. Suddenly it turned on its back and rolled, legs kicking, and then it thrust itself over, leapt to its feet, neighed and cantered away among the trees.

John shivered for an instant, and then pulled away more determinedly.

They soon reached the road. This time, he reasoned, they would not be so stupid, and he pushed on steadily, doggedly, defiantly.

They drove in silence for quite some time, climbing steadily up over the mountains that they had crossed the day before, creeping cautiously down ravines where the road twisted and snaked and finally crossed a dry, rock-strewn stream bed, only to struggle upwards yet again.

And although he kept his eyes open to see just where they had gone wrong the day before, consulting the map every mile or so, he still missed it. He could not see where he could possibly have turned off, for the road was the only one that crawled over the endless mountains, and yet they were soon in places that they had not seen the day before.

They seemed to climb even higher, until the sea was a far-off sheet of silver that glinted at a dizzy depth below them. The road twisted and turned, zigzagging ever closer to the sky. There were not even any sheep or donkeys this high up. Even the flowers had changed. Now only a few low plants huddled close to the ground, hiding from the wind that had sprung up and which scoured the heights. He even had to pull the windows up to protect them from the chill.

They came to a bend and they both drew their breath in in surprise. The whole island lay at their feet. To right and left, the sea stretched out to infinity, this glinting frame of the patch of land to which they clung so perilously. Closer in, fold after fold of hill and mountain receded in graded shades of blues and purples slashed by the great dark gashes of valleys. On a crest far off to the right, there ran a line of broken humps, jagged outcrops of stone, the ruins of those who had conquered this land before time began.

Their hotel had to be somewhere down there, John concluded as he studied the map.

They drove on slowly, the road curling around the peak on which they had stood a few moments earlier. They dropped into folds in the hills, climbed again, turned and turned and turned again so that the mountains always changed place, changed position relative to each other, like encircling giants dancing endlessly around them.

She reached over and lay her hand on his. He turned to look, and she smiled.

"I'm sorry, too," she said. "But things will be all right now."

He smiled and laid his hand on hers.

They drove on silently among the poppies, the thorns and the rock-strewn land.

"He was a strange man," John said eventually.

"He certainly was," Jane added.

Silence fell again as they moved steadily forwards.

"There was something about him," he said at length.

"He was ...," she hesitated, "too ... persuasive, too personal. He knew too much. He always answered your questions before you'd asked them."

"Anyway," he concluded, "we did see something of the real country."

He fell silent as he nursed the car between a particularly bad series of pot-holes and round a very tight bend. He gripped the wheel, his tongue caught between his teeth in concentration.

"If you came down here too fast," he warned, gesturing to his right where the hill side dropped away steeply down to the sea, and where a small shrine stood at the roadside, "you would ..."

"It's the same," she interrupted hoarsely.

"No, it isn't," he shouted, and then he re-assured her, more patiently and more plausibly, "they're probably all the same."

He stopped the car, and they stood at the side of the

road, examining the shrine. It was like the other, the same size, the same glass door, the same hideous icon, with the same sanctimonious smirk, the same gaudy clothing, the same red lips and gilded teeth, the same air of tawdry smugness. In fact, this picture was even more offensive because it was less rusted, less faded, less eaten away by time.

"But the bottle is the same, and so is the saucer."

"It isn't," he said, "Don't be silly. This one is new. The outside is all painted. There are still flowers in the bottle."

Jane turned and walked slowly to her left, and then she stopped, leaned, virtually collapsed against a large boulder that stood at the side of the road.

"See," he called out after her, "this one hasn't been here long. There's a wreath here." He brandished the twisted tangle of dried leaves and silver paper that he had picked up at the foot of the post, took it to show her.

They both stared at the track that led away down the hill side.

"It's not possible," he shouted. "It is not possible."

He turned and raced back to the car. He turned the key and made the engine scream. He let the clutch in violently, and the car bounced forward, the wheels spinning and throwing up great clouds of dust. A wheel dropped into a pot-hole and the whole car juddered, but he accelerated even more, spinning the steering wheel, crashing the gear lever into reverse, bouncing the car out of the hole, and then forcing the lever back into first gear and forcing the car forwards.

"Come on," he yelled at Jane who was still standing by the boulder, "come on. Get in. We'll get this sorted out."

Before she had closed the door, he had let the clutch in, causing the car to leap forward, ripping the exhaust off on the lip where the track met the road.

"Serves them right," he screamed and accelerated away.

* * *

The turquoise boats swayed lazily on the swell of time. A large white goat stood upright on its back legs, its front legs resting on the trunk of an olive tree as it strained just a little higher, struggling to attain those leaves which were just out of reach.

A dog lay in the middle of the road. It did not even bother to get up, and they had to drive around it. As they passed, the tail swished once or twice in welcome.

"Hello," a voice called out from the doorway, "how nice to see you. Come in. Sit down. Please."

From out of the shadow a man stepped. He was tall and lean, with long, black hair and a drooping moustache that curled around his lips. He stood aside, stretched out his arm to invite them to enter, bowed and smiled. There was a dull glimmer of gold in the shadow.

"What is this game?" John shouted, shaking with rage and impotence.

"Please," he said, "would you like a nice, cool drink? It is a hot day."

Then he picked up an apron made of some coarse, striped material and tied it around his waist. He took a cloth and hurried to sweep a few crumbs from a table and to dust the seats of two chairs.

"No! No!" John shouted.

He turned to the door.

"Maria! Maria!" he called.

"No! No!" he screamed, beside himself with rage.

"Don't worry," he soothed him, "don't worry. Many people get lost. No problem. It is so easy to get lost, and maps are hard to read." He smiled, his gold tooth glinting as if deliberately, mischievously in the shadow of the room.

"We didn't get lost," John argued, "the map is wrong."

"When you get lost, the map is always wrong. But now you have found your way here, so it is well."

"No!" John shouted. "We are not staying here. We want to see the temples."

"But we have a temple here," the man protested, his voice driving deep into John's head like some excruciating pain, and he pointed out across the sea to the headland. John had to look, despite himself. It must have been that the sun was at a different angle, for the temple was quite clear. You could see the pillars and even parts of the roof, a massive structure in white stone that soared above the rocky spit.

"They say," the voice continued, "that the gods used to swim out from here in the evening. The gods would swim straight into the setting sun, and then would arrive at that headland. Then they used to wait to watch the sun dip into the sea, and then they used to make love. All night!" He glanced at Jane, smiled, raised his eyebrows in feigned surprise. She turned away from his look.

"That is why we build temples only in the places where gods make love. They are our desires made into stone."

Maria appeared, carrying a tray on which there were two glasses and a pitcher of lemon juice. She glanced shyly from under her eyelids, smiling uncertainly like a timid child. Her clothing rustled and sparkled as she crossed the room, a frail figure adorned in bright, flashing silks and gold. The ice clinked in the pitcher and the bangles tinkled like tiny bells around her wrists. She smelt of the sea, of the night breeze, of the musk of the horse and the dried perfume of flowers.

"No! No!" he protested, as he found he could not help but guess at the body under the flowing silks, could not help but imagine the burning touch of her flesh as they galloped through the moonlit waves, the wild, trilling laugh, the piercing, primitive whinny of a horse.

"That is why we have such marvellous gods. Gods of the sun and of the moon, gods of the earth, of the sea, of the rain, gods of flowers, gods of birds, gods who ride recklessly on the winds, others who ride at night along the sands, gods ..."

"No! No!" John shouted, jumping to his feet. And he stood motionless in the shade of the trees.

"No!" he shouted again. "We do not have enough time."

"No," he agreed, "we do not have enough time. But it

is the only thing we do have, so we must use it wisely. We do not cry for the time before we were born. We must not mourn for the time after we have gone. There is no time outside ourselves."

"No!" he shouted, fighting desperately, "we are going."

He turned and hurried away, pushing Jane in front of him. As they got back to the car, the dog walked slowly up to them, his tail wagging lazily in expectation. John did not notice, pushing past and without thinking lifting a foot to drive the dog away. It stopped, considered the two visitors for a moment, and then flopped down in the dust again and closed its eyes.

"We are going home," John said decisively when they were safely in the car.

"You are wrong, my friends. You must not chase the false gods of others."

John let the clutch in violently, and the tyres scrabbled at the dust. In a hideous noise of the racing engine, and grating gears and slipping tyres they roared out past the hotel, just missing the dog which had not moved from its spot.

"We are going home," he said.

Jane sat silently, tense and anxious as he drove recklessly along. They shot out of the track back onto the main road, turning left, away from the mountains, away from the road they should have taken, back down towards the town from where they had started.

They drove on steadily, slowly rediscovering peace and humility in the vast, uncaring emptiness. On one side the sea stretched for ever, an unbroken sheet around the world in time and space. On the other, hills receded in layer upon layer, becoming paler and paler until you could not tell whether it was land or sky.

It was beautiful. If the gods had lived anywhere, then it had to be here.

"You know," he said after a long while, "perhaps we were stupid. We should have gone to see his temple."

He turned towards her and saw her smile.

"While we had the chance," he added.

"Perhaps we should," she said, and she lifted her hand to her nose, seeking the faint trace of olive-wood that lingered, feeling the dry scorch of his lips.

He slowed down, and they held hands contentedly as the car was eased gently along.

The dark mass of a nearby ridge sloped down towards them, ending in a sharp rise, a small plateau and then a sheer drop to a valley floor a thousand feet below. The valley could be glimpsed, a blue sea of haze amidst darker mountains that receded, paler and paler, from green to blue to grey and even white, until the final horizon melted into the sky. Here and there the darker finger of a cypress tree stood out, here and there a jagged mass of white rocks jutted from the earth.

They looked out at the line of low headlands stretched out behind them, knotted white fingers of rock that tried in vain to seize the sea. Further off, an island drifted almost imperceptibly in the mist, a crouched mass of land with, on its summit, a temple.

"John," she screamed and drew in her breath

involuntarily.

The track turned back abruptly, seemed for a moment to lean upon the sky itself, before it veered away from the void and climbed, ever more steeply, ever upwards.

"John," she screamed in fear, and then added, quite redundantly, "there's a bend!"

The front wheel dropped into a pot-hole and the car shuddered and slewed around. The car lurched and complained, and the tyres scrabbled for a hold on the dusty surface. There was the startling, thin crash of glass as a bottle rolled off the back seat and shattered on the floor. For a moment they remained balanced precariously on the very edge.

For a second he hesitated.

And then she screamed, a long-drawn, piercing scream.

* * *

A brilliant scarab settled for a second on the windscreen, only to be swept off by the wipers. He must have turned them on in his frantic movements and now they alone broke the silence with the rhythmic grating and scratching of their blades which gradually, inexorably slowed and then stopped.

* * *

"Horses," he mumbled, "I can hear horses."

"There's somebody coming. I can hear horses."

He stood expectantly in the road.

At the edge of the road, where the mountainside fell

steeply away, there was a small shrine.

The shrine was clearly new. The icon was still bright and shining, and its colours were as crude and gaudy as they must have been when it came from the factory. The robe and headband were a bright, metallic blue, the collar a violent scarlet, the flesh of the face and neck and hands a strangely artificial pink, the halo, the fingernails, the eyelids, the whites of the eyes, the lips and even one of the teeth were brashly gilded, the background was a shimmering silver like the sea.

The shrine stood upright on a new stake at the base of which a few flowers still fluttered drily in the wind. A card was wedged between the strands of wire that held the flowers, and he picked it up to read the inscription. Inside the shrine, the wilting heads of a few daisies, identical to those which flowered all around on the hill-side, bent over the neck of a wine bottle. A saucer held the remains of a candle and a few spent matches.

"This one is new," John called defiantly, obstinately.

Then he took a few steps back, almost stumbling as he tried to locate the sound.

"There's somebody coming," he said. "I can hear horses."

Six grey horses slowly appeared from the track that turned off and led down the valley on the right. The noise of their hoofs resounded on the baked earth and rumbled like thunder around the mountains. A frail figure swathed in flowing silks was perched on the lead horse, calling commands in a high-pitched voice. She called out strange words, she whistled to urge the horses on as they struggled to pull their load over the lip from the track onto the main road. Slowly, the low, four-wheeled cart appeared, the enormous wheels digging deep into the dust as it was dragged forward. A man stood on the cart, hauling on ropes to make sure that as the cart tipped at an angle the cargo of two coffins did not slide off into the dirt.

He lifted the bodies up onto the cart and arranged them as best he could among the silk linings. The boxes were then propped up, as is the way in the mountains, not quite upright, but almost so.

The man took a stake and a sledge-hammer from the cart. He drove the metal stake firmly down into the ground, and then on top fastened a small shrine that he had brought. It was a cheap, tinny thing, with a flashy picture on poorly made gilded cardboard. An old saucer held a candle and he gathered a few flowers from the hill side and put them in a bottle filled with water. He lit the candle, leaving the spent match in the saucer, and closed the door of the shrine. He then went back to the cart and took a small wreath which he propped against the stake. He stepped back to examine his work and seemed well enough pleased. Then he smiled as he read again the words written in clumsy letters on the card: "To Travellers".

He threw back his head and laughed, the gold tooth flashing in the scorching sun.

They were ready to begin the slow journey back. The horses moved off, the trinkets with which they were adorned clinking, the resonant beat of their hoofs pounding in the heads of those they bore away.

As they came into town, the driver took up a more seemly position on the box, and the man walked behind. They went down the hill in front of the school, and on past the church where they came out on the street that ran along the sea. The street was already busy with people on holiday, some lying lazily in the sun, others hurrying about buying souvenirs of what they had never done or seen, fobbed off with specious baubles as substitutes for reality.

In front of the car hire office, a man was loading luggage for a timid looking couple who were watching him apprehensively.

As they approached, they turned to stare for a moment, but then they all went into the shop.

It was just, he was explaining, the way of the men of the mountains, just that they thought there should be one last chance. You could see them talking in the shop. You could see him laugh, you could see her fascinated, horror-struck face.

As they drew up in front of the shop, the mourner turned and, surprised by her earnest stare, lifted his hat, bowed and smiled. And then he laughed, the gold tooth flashing in the morning sun.

"But you go now," he was saying. "You go or you will miss the chance to swim."

They came out of the office, blinking for a few seconds in the brilliant light. Then, despite herself, she looked up at the coffins, peered in among the clouds of silk.

And then she screamed, a long-drawn, piercing scream.

* * *

Suddenly they were out of the valley. A couple of boats, brightly painted in a turquoise colour that was almost identical to the colour of the water, rocked lazily a few yards off-shore. To their left there was a large field, perhaps an orchard, with orderly rows of trees underneath which were clouds of brilliant poppies and lemon daisies swaying in the breeze. Donkeys and goats grazed quietly, their bells tinkling gently as they moved between the trees.

"Is this it?" she asked.

A dog lay in the middle of the road. As they approached, it stood up, wagged its tail and walked towards them expectantly.

"It must be," John replied.

They called out from under the trees, but nobody came.

They walked along the beach for a while, but still they saw nobody. The sun was beginning to sink towards a headland on the far side of the bay, behind a temple that stood proudly right on the top of the hill, dominating the sea and the land around.

"We should see the temple," they said, and, as there was nobody about, they slipped naked into the sea.

They swam effortlessly, carried by the water, gently rocked from swell to swell, rhythmically striking out for the setting sun. It was so easy in the warm, salty water that they could have swum forever.

When they clambered out onto the headland, the sun had almost sunk into the sea. It was obvious now that it was just a trick of the light, for there was no temple at all, just a huge outcrop of rocks thrown haphazardly around by unknown forces.

They stood close together, leaning against the warm rock, watching the sun sink slowly into the glistening sea. A slight breeze caught the strands of her hair, blowing them across his face, and for a moment he caught the smell of olive-wood and thyme.

As the sun was setting, they lay on the ground, amongst the tangle of flowers, and made love. At peace at last.

"Do you know," he said as he looked at her, "do you know why they used to build temples?"

"Yes," she answered, "to mark where gods come to make love." And then she threw back her head and laughed. "Why?" she asked, "do you want them to build one for us?"

And they kissed and laughed, and the setting sun sank below the horizon, imparting to everything -to the land, the sea, the temple, their hair, their skin, and, as they laughed and kissed, imparting especially to their teeth- a glorious golden glow.

※ ※ ※

The House

A clash of cultures

The door slammed closed behind her. She turned slowly and stared for a moment at the bare weathered planks.

A gust of wind must have sprung up, even though the morning seemed quite still. |Far down below in the valley, blue smoke spiralled lazily from the chimneys. These trembling lines might sometimes curl in sinuous whorls, but then they would straighten, flatten and blend into the misty haze that stretched down the valley to the glistening sea.

On the mountain, the wind seemed always to blow, sometimes unpredictably, sometimes perversely. Even on a summer's day, with no cloud in the sky, the wind could suddenly hurl a handful of cutting rain, causing the circling buzzards to mew their shrill complaints, the old ewes to huddle behind a protective tussock, and the impotent farmer to shake his head.

"It doesn't matter now anyway," she thought.

She looked out over the land. She knew each field,

each hill, each house. As she gazed regretfully, she recited the rosary of their names. Farther off, over the plain, a rainbow shone, announcing rain for later.

Black clouds slowly massed on the horizon, advanced over the sea that changed -the alchemist's despair- from glistening gold to dullest lead. A squall howled at the chimney. She shivered and pulled her shawl close.

"It is time," she said.

The sun slipped behind a cloud.

The hoarfrost that lingered in the hollows no longer sparkled, and the drops of ice that clung to the yellow blades of grass in the stream beds no longer glinted like diamonds.

She reached for the latch. But there was no need: everything was as it should be.

Her eyes watered, perhaps because of her age, perhaps because of sorrow, perhaps simply because of the wind that snatched at her thin wisps of grey hair. Then she turned away and headed up the track that led to the mountains.

* * *

The clock chimed half past twelve.

In the village pub the landlord threw some logs on the fire, listened to the wind.

"Sounds like a storm," he said.

Several voices rose from the huddle of old men by the fire.

"It has been a bad winter."

"There's still snow on the tops."

"It's a long time since we've had such a winter."

Silence settled gently over them again, like the snow falling on the mountains.

The door burst open.

"There's no smoke."

"Shut the door," they grumbled, as the wind cut at their ankles.

"There's no smoke," the newcomer shouted again.

He pulled the landlord urgently by the sleeve. He opened the door and pointed up the mountain.

They stared silently upwards to the house perched high above.

"We'd better go up," one of them said.

"Do you see?" another insisted. "There's still snow on the tops."

"We shall see," the landlord said reflectively, "we shall see."

* * *

The door closed. They had all come to see, and now they had gone. The house was quiet at last, except for the wind, of course, which rushed around gleefully, taking possession, whistling and whispering in every corner, just like the old women who had just left.

They turned up their collars, pulled their coats more tightly around themselves, and set out on the path down to the village. They shivered and looked up at the bald, bleak hills. Black clouds lumbered in from the sea like unspoken threats, and there was still snow on the tops. Others would die before long, they thought, and hurried away.

They held a service in the chapel graveyard.

"Ashes to ashes and dust ..."

The words were snatched by the wind and spread with the drizzle over the roofs of the village.

If their thoughts wandered, it was not that they lacked respect, it was that it was cold, and the wind and the rain were cutting through their Sunday best. But they stood and tried to remember.

She had been born in that house high up on the mountain, as had her mother, and her grandmother, and her great-grandmother and so on since before people remembered.

The old women in the village used to gossip sometimes, saying how strange it was, how shameful, and they would cackle their lascivious suspicions, for, from generation to generation, the women of the house had borne a child out of wedlock. And nobody had ever known for sure who the father was. And only daughters had ever been born.

Now it was time for her daughter to return. She had been away for some time, away nobody knew where. From time to time, she had been seen, early in the morning, coming on foot across the mountains, or leaving the house in the evening and disappearing silently and quickly into the mist.

But now she would come back, for her mother had gone and the winter was lingering on and the house was getting cold. And, besides, that was the way it had always been.

Sometimes they thought that she had come, for they could have sworn that they had seen lights in the windows, that they had been woken by noises. In the morning they would go up, only to find the house empty. Perhaps it had just been the full moon. Perhaps it had just been the owls hooting.

The winter ground on, taking its tithe of the old, reluctantly conceding life to the fruits of last summer's rapid passions. The wind howled through the valley, chilling the blood with its bitter threats. The old stared grimly into their glasses, and for the thousandth time calculated who should be next.

Springtime dawdled maliciously. There was still snow on the mountains when the ewes started lambing: the foxes were desperately hungry, and the crows, more vicious and even more persistent, hopped and squawked and pecked greedily at the sight of the new-born lambs.

In the village they waited for her to come home to look after the house, the house that she had had from her mother, her grandmother, her great-grandmother and so on, from age to age, for ever and ever.

* * *

At last there came those long evenings when the wind caressed and encouraged the lovers who had gone up the mountain.

In the pub the old men shuffled their feet and thought how much more tragic it would be to die in summer than in winter.

The door opened and a surge of warm, perfumed air came in to taunt them.

"Good evening".

Their eyes were lifted silently.

"A visitor," one grumbled.

"Already," another complained.

"Glorious evening, isn't it?" the tourist added.

More reliable than the cuckoo is this harbinger of summer.

The door opened again and a surge of a different perfume rushed in.

"Oh," she drawled, "what a simply lovely old pub."

And she strolled round the room, so shamelessly examining everything. She smiled so nicely as she eased past the men by the fire, and the wake of perfume made them sniff surreptitiously like well-bred hounds, and the swirl of coloured silk made them lift their downcast eyes, and its gentle rustle thundered in their ears.

"Landlord," one of the men growled, "Visitors!" And he swore under his breath and he drank slowly from his glass.

"Simply lovely," she gushed. "I say, do let's stay here."

"Good evening," the landlord said in the old language as he came in from the back.

"Oh," she cried, "how quaint. We really must stay."

* * *

So they stayed.

They greeted the peasants who were sweating in the

fields, and took the curt nod and a silent curse as signs of rural dignity and restraint.

They marvelled at the beauty of the screaming buzzard that circled and wheeled and soared majestically as it desperately scavenged for rotting flesh.

They were thrilled to see the gaunt figure of the poet-priest striding over the mountains, but they didn't know he was grimly searching for that place so desolate that his soul's anguish might finally be at home.

They ambled along the lanes or by the sea, and had picnics and watched birds through their binoculars, and the sun shone and everything was simply lovely.

And in the evenings they sat in the pub and drank whisky and wine and smiled and nodded amiably. And her perfume aroused in the old men what they wished were memories, but were really only yesterday's dreams.

And the women squinted sidelong at her as she sauntered smilingly by. And every word the visitors said was heard, and every thing they did was seen, and all was repeated and remembered.

And the tourist came to dream of a different life. He would come to live in this place, simply, naturally, as did the villagers, with no problems, with no worries. He would write novels, take photographs, raise chickens, a cow, a goat, some geese. Perhaps he would go to evening classes to learn pottery. And he would learn the old language of poets and peasants.

"Although," he conceded to his wife in the pub that evening, "It can't be much fun in winter."

"Goodness, no," she shrieked.

The landlord listened and stared in silence.

"But then," the tourist argued, "we wouldn't have to be here all the time. We could always nip back down for weekends, catch up on the theatres, do a spot of shopping."

He turned back to the landlord.

"That's what we thought," he explained, "I mean, it's not the end of the world here, is it?"

And they both laughed heartily, and had another drink.

The landlord smiled thinly, shrugged and moved away.

"Besides," the tourist concluded, glancing around carefully, whispering to his wife so that the locals wouldn't hear, "it's so cheap here."

* * *

Every day the tourist planned, and every day the plans became more detailed, more grandiose. There was only one problem.

"You don't know of a house for sale?" he asked the landlord.

"There's nothing for sale around here," he answered.

But one night they rushed excitedly into the pub.

"We walked up the mountain today," they explained.

"There's nice," said the landlord.

"And we found an old abandoned house."

"Just up above the village," his wife added, "with a

marvellous view."

"Has it been abandoned for long?" the tourist asked. "It looked in quite good condition."

"You see," he explained, "we don't mind doing something up."

"There are no abandoned houses on the mountain," the landlord replied sternly.

"Excuse me," said an old man who reached over for his glass.

"But you can see it from here. Just up on the mountain, looking down on the whole valley as far as the sea."

"The house is not abandoned," the landlord said.

"Ah," said the tourist, and he sat and sipped at his whisky.

* * *

"But it's very small," she argued the next day as they sat yet again on the garden wall and looked out over the land.

It really was a marvellous view. In front of the house the valley ran down to the plain, and the silver sea glinted in the background. To the right, a peninsula stretched out to the horizon; to the left were bays and coves. Behind the house were the mountains with their old lanes and walls like cobwebs that reached out into every corner of the land. You could have thought that the whole country was spread out at the feet of the house as if it was its servant, as if doing homage.

"But we could extend it," he argued.

"And it's full of potential," he insisted.

And she had to concede.

* * *

When they arrived at the pub that evening, she wandered over to the fire where the old men huddled. She stood and warmed herself, bestowing gracious smiles and playful little gurgles of pleasure on their stony faces.

"Could I have a whisky, please?" the tourist asked. He turned, raised a glass and an eyebrow to offer her a drink.

She smiled.

"And a glass of red wine, please," he added.

He paused for a moment, waited until the landlord had put the drinks on the bar.

"And does anybody live there at the moment?" he asked, as he sorted through his money.

"No. She died this spring."

"Ah," he said more hopefully. "I am sorry," he said, trying not to smile. He looked up. "Won't you have a drink with us?"

The tourist raised his glass.

"Who owns the house now then?"

"Her daughter."

"And where does she live?"

"Nobody knows," the landlord answered. "But she'll be back when she knows about her mother."

"She doesn't know her mother is dead?" the tourist's

wife gasped in horror. "How will you tell her when she arrives?"

"There'll be no need to tell her. She will know."

"But how will she know if you haven't told her?"

"They know many things," he added. "We shall see soon enough. And anyway," he added with perfect logic, "if she won't know, she won't come, will she?"

The tourist and his wife sat thoughtfully at the bar. Now and again they whispered to each other, but mainly they just sat.

* * *

"And it's very run down," she objected, as they peeped in at the windows.

"And it leaks," she complained as they stood in the porch to shelter for a moment from a sudden shower.

The wind pulled at their clothes and hair. She shivered and crossed her arms to keep out the chill.

"What on earth was that?" she cried.

"The wind," he said, reassuring her and himself. "A door must have slammed in the wind."

"But it was right behind us," she said.

They stared at the bare boards of the door and at the heavy iron latch.

"Let's go," she said. "It's not for sale, anyway, so there's no point in dreaming."

* * *

"It must have been open," she explained patiently to the landlord that evening. "The wind sprang up suddenly and there was this big bang from right behind us. I can't think what else it can have been."

"You opened the door?" the landlord asked, shocked at such behaviour.

"Certainly not," retorted the tourist. "The door must have been open, although we didn't notice it."

As his voice rose, the old men by the fire became quiet, and his words fell on a silent, attentive room. The landlord glanced towards the old men, hesitated for a moment, searching for his words.

"It couldn't have been," he said.

He paused, stopped. The old men all started talking together suddenly.

"Excuse me," he said. "There is somebody who needs serving." And he hurried away.

The animated voices chattered incomprehensibly by the fire. The tourist and his wife sat silently. Now and again they turned to look round the room, and it seemed that each time they did so the old men, who had clearly been staring at them, averted their eyes.

The tourist waited. He watched thoughtfully as the landlord served other customers, piled logs on the fire, washed up the glasses.

He remembered having been advised that country folk didn't like to be rushed.

"So you don't think," the tourist asked some thirty minutes later, "that she would like to sell the house?"

"She will live in her house," he answered firmly. "She will live in her house and she will die in her house, like her mother and her grandmother and her great-grandmother and her mother before her."

"I see," said the tourist, quite exasperated. "But you don't even know if she will come back here."

"She will come back," the landlord affirmed.

"When?"

"Soon. Soon."

"But you don't know when?"

"No. Not exactly."

"But you are certain she will be back."

"Oh yes. She will be back. Very soon now." And a half-smile ghosted across his face.

* * *

Despite the predictions of the landlord, she did not come back. The tourist's wife was quite relieved, for she had already tired of rural pastimes, and had exhausted her interest in little birds and wild flowers. She spent her days lying -naked, so the village women hissed- in a sheltered spot out of the wind and reading books and magazines.

He went back up the mountain every day to look at the house. He walked around outside; he looked in through the windows; he sat for hours in the garden by the stream. But he never found the door open and concluded that they must have been mistaken on that earlier day, that the wind and the noise must just have startled them.

His passion was frustrated: the object of his desire stood before him, undefended and yet untouched, not even deigning to protect itself from his lust.

If at least she had come back, even if only to refuse his offer, to live there herself, then he could have left in peace. But the vulnerability of the house, its very openness taunted him. And he would never know whether she would have accepted. She obviously didn't want it that much or she would look after it. Perhaps it would have been his, he argued as he climbed up the mountain for the last time.

He should just have gone in. And even if it wasn't open, then it certainly wouldn't have taken much to open it.

Now it was time to go back to the city, and he would never know.

When he arrived at the garden gate he stood for a moment, looking over the country spread out at his feet, There was only the sound of the kite crying, the wind slipping through the long grass, the urgent beating of his heart.

The door was slightly open.

"Hello?" he called, "is there anybody there?"

"Hello?" he called again, "I want to talk to you. I need to talk to you."

He pushed the door gently. The hinges creaked and the door swung slowly farther open.

The tourist stared into the room, but he could see nobody. He hesitated for a minute and then, warily, he went in.

With the sunlight streaming in through the open door, he could see the room quite well. Everything seemed in order. The furniture was all in place and the house was clean, as if somebody had just gone out. But the clock on the mantel shelf was stopped at half past twelve.

"Hello," he called, "is there anybody home?"

He thought he heard something, a noise like that of whispering or laughing, like a kind of hissing whistle. He turned. The room was empty.

The tourist started to climb the stairs. He was agitated and nervous, although he didn't know why. Although he had come to see the house for the last time, he felt as if something was just beginning. He had forgotten his wife who was waiting down at the pub. He had forgotten everything.

There was only one room upstairs: a large room with a bed in the centre. The room was full of light coming in through the door from the stairs. He looked shyly at the bed because the room was somehow full of the presence of women. He sat down on the bed for fear of falling. He could not have said whether the whistling sound was coming from inside his body, along with the thump of his heartbeat, or from outside, along with the incessant hissing of the wind. The sound became louder and louder and he felt quite drunk, quite ill. He decided to go, but he felt so weak, so sleepy.

A shadow fell on the bed. He opened his eyes. There was somebody in the room, standing by the door. He couldn't see very well because of the light that was coming from behind the shape, but there was somebody there, there was no doubt about that. He wanted to get up, but his body would not obey.

"Who is that?"

There was no answer. The shape came closer. There

was a great gust of wind and the door slammed closed.

* * *

When they went up to look for him, the door was closed. They went in, but there was nobody in the house. There was no sign of him outside either. They went back down for more help, but even when they came back with most of the villagers, they still found nothing. At nightfall they had to abandon their search.

They resumed the next morning, but even though the police brought their dogs, they found no trace.

* * *

They never discovered what happened to the tourist. The newspapers, of course, had suggested all sorts of things. In the village they simply said "We'll see."

"We'll see," they said as they sat around in the pub.

"We'll see," and they drank deeply.

* * *

Down in the valley, the villagers hurried unquestioningly through the end of the summer, scrabbling for their meagre harvests, fattening the animals they would soon kill, coupling self-consciously in brief minutes of rare desire. And they hoarded these interludes of warmth in their bodies and their minds to protect them from the wind.

For the wind was only rarely absent, rarely silent. It drove inexorably in from the sea, hissing up the valley to the mountains. Sometimes it urged great shrouds of rain before it; sometimes white clouds scudded romantically across the sky; sometimes, although not very often, it sighed and caressed, making even senile horses grazing peacefully in the fields whinny with a pale memory of delight.

Usually it just blew, quarrelling petulantly with the house high up on the mountain, gnawing doggedly at this bone of contention.

The villagers struggled on, impotent, tied to this land, like a man and wife who have long been married. Habit and necessity have made them blind to both the good and the ill in their partner. The sun appeared rarely, and a smile was rarer than the sun. Yet it did appear, and now and again a thrush would perch on the highest branch and sing, and now and again harebells danced in every hedge, and now and again they remembered the better days of their youth.

Then black clouds gathered. And their days were full of bitterness and bile, and at times life was so empty of joy that strangers might ask whether it was worth the unremitting, crushing struggle to maintain it.

But they cling like limpets, and somehow find their sustenance on this barren rock. And somehow, through being nailed to such a cruel fate, their struggle brings some begrudged dignity. As resilient as weeds, they close their drab petals and huddle, shivering, until the next warm kiss.

* * *

The landlord threw some logs on the fire, listened to the wind.

"Sounds like a storm," he said.

"It has been a bad winter," one old man said.

"There's still snow on the tops," another added.

The door burst open.

"There's smoke in the house."

They all hurried to the door and looked up at the mountain. A thin trail of smoke rose from the chimney of the house, hesitated for a moment, and then was snatched away by the wind.

She settled into the house and lived as her mother and her grandmother had done before her: alone and without saying a word.

One day, as the farmers hurried to plant their wet fields, as the ewes fought off the crows with a courage they themselves could not understand, as the old men sat round the fire and were glad that winter had spared them, the noise of a child crying came down on the wind, spreading over the village like the blessing of Spring.

The old women smiled and chuckled. The men lifted their heads to the mountain and their eyes twinkled.

A daughter had been born in the house.

❀ ❀ ❀

ABOUT THE AUTHOR

I am originally from South Wales, but I was brought up in England. I studied at the University of Leeds and at the Université de Dijon. I currently live in Wales with my wife, Ann.

For many years I lectured at universities in France, Canada and Switzerland. At the same time, I wrote short stories, articles, plays and scripts for television documentaries. Books published over the years range from tongue-in-cheek political satire to an introduction to Dylan Thomas, with a critical anthology of the poetry of Dafydd ap Gwilym along the way.

I have been invited to give talks at venues ranging from American Graduation Ceremonies to Community Arts Associations. Such talks have been on subjects ranging from Dafydd ap Gwilym to Dylan Thomas and to George Catlin and his interest in the "Welsh Indians".

Nine of my short stories are collected in this volume.

This volume is available from booksellers, from Amazon and from the author at gweithdy@yahoo.com.

Printed in Great Britain
by Amazon